And You'd Better Not Tell

And You'd Better Not Tell

Nina Foxx

Clever Vixen Media

Seattle

ALSO BY NINA FOXX

Dippin' My Spoon

Get Some Love

Going Buck Wild

Marrying Up

Just Short of Crazy

No Girl Needs A Husband Seven Days A Week

Momma: Gone

Catfish

A Letter for My Mother (editor)

AS CONTRIBUTOR

Can't Help the Way That I Feel

Do The Write Thing: 7 Steps to Publishing Success

Wanderlust: Erotic Travel Tales

Ley Lines

AS CYNNAMON FOSTER

Southern Comfort

Eastern Spice

Northern Passion

For my girls, Sydney and Kai

And my young men, Collier, Drake & Ellison

May you all respect yourselves and others.

Throughout history, it has been the inaction of those who could have acted; the indifference of those who should have known better; the silence of the voice of justice when it mattered most; that has made it possible for evil to triumph.

— Haile Selassie

PROLOGUE

As far as Dante was concerned, fifth period lunch was the best there was. It wasn't too early so that you felt like you'd just had breakfast, but it wasn't so late that you would be starving before the bell rang and were forced to eat whatever it was they were serving and passing off as food. Fifth period lunch was like Baby Bear and his porridge, just right. A girl walked past them and every eye followed.

"You see what I mean, man?" Dante spoke the question aloud. But none of his friends answered verbally. They just nodded. They all had a mutual understanding of the reason they stood outside the lunchroom just before the bell rang every day, and the reason had nothing to do with the food. From here, they could take in all the girls.

As always, Dante stood outside the lunchroom, his back to the lockers that lined the wall. His friends lined up beside him. If they spoke, it was in hushed tones and abbreviated sentences, often just one word filled with hawk-like judgment, an inventory of everything about everyone that passed in front of them. They were not there to talk. They were there to *see*.

As kings of the school, Dante and his friends got to check things out as much as they wanted, like watching from the vantage points of majestic thrones that were just a few steps higher than everyone else.

Mr. Jones, a guidance counselor walked past and the boys froze as if immobility would make them invisible. He made eye contact with the boys but did not shoo them away. Instead, he gave them a quick nod, his dreadlocks flowing around his head like a mane. The nod was not necessarily one of approval, but one that said, "I see what you're up to."

A seventh grader stopped next to them.

"Hey, Gym Class." Gym class was a great basketball player, but it wasn't his time to be king yet, that title belonged to eighth graders only. He hadn't earned a name.

"Hey, Dante, wassup? Your kicks are hot," he said. The boy was trying to sound cool, only he didn't sound cool at all.

All eyes turned to Dante and his neck prickled a little from the heat that was rising there. Judging eyes turned to him now, wanting to know what Dante was going to do. The way he handled the situation was everything, and this definitely was a *situation*. Depending on what he said, or didn't say, the rest of the year could be ruined. Dante could find himself in a new position in the middle school pecking order, possibly one he didn't want.

Dante took a deep breath and turned his head only slightly toward the boy. He flared his nose and glared, hard. The boy drew back as if Dante had hit him, involuntarily taking two steps in the other direction. The other boys smirked in approval. The bell rang, and one of the boys gave Dante a high-five.

They all stepped inside the lunchroom, then made their way to the table, their table. The seventh grader didn't follow.

"Damn." Dante spoke to no one in particular. Like the rest of the boys at his table, they all held their breath as Joyce walked by.

"Why are the new girls always the finest?" one of the boys said. "She came two weeks ago."

"I wanna know where she came from and if there are more like her," Dante's voice was low, his eyes glued to Joyce.

Joyce was fine. She had this thing that the other girls didn't have, a thing that lit up the whole room when she entered. That girl could be as quiet as a mouse, but her presence would just take over, drawing all eyes in her direction. No one could put a finger as to why; it wasn't necessarily her long, toned legs that clearly shown through her yoga pants, or that she had started growing breasts already, but all of the parts being together made a package that outshone everyone else.

"Damn?" Tyson shoved Dante. "That's all you can say? All talk and no action."

"I ain't trying to get at that." Dante tried to play it off. Joyce was the hottest girl he'd ever seen. She wore her long hair in big braids that hung down past her shoulders, and although they were in middle school, she already had curves that were headed toward what

Dante was used to seeing on high school girls. All any of them had done so far was admire her from afar; they had no idea how to approach her and Dante wasn't sure if he wanted to. He had no idea what he would do if he did, so for now, just dreaming of her was enough.

"You're supposed to let her know you're interested. Let her know you're here, Man." Tyson egged him on.

"Whatever. What do you know about it?" Dante turned around and tried to shake Joyce out of his thoughts, but the way she walked kept creeping back into his mind and made it almost impossible for him to think of something else. He couldn't concentrate. "I don't see you stepping to her."

"She's not my type, or I would." Tyson paused and flipped open his school schedule. "My older brother tells me all about women. I've been watching him for years. Rest assured, when I'm ready, I'm gonna be smooth because I will have learned from the best. He says that women want you to be assertive. You're supposed to let them know that you're the man and they're the woman."

"That's dumb. I'm pretty sure she already knows she's a girl. Look at the way she walks. And that hair. It just flows in the wind behind her when she passes", Dante said. He rubbed his hands on his sweat pants.

"You're stupid. That's just woman tricks. That shit ain't real." Tyson laughed and the rest of the boys at the table laughed with him.

Dante's face got hot. "That's just mean."

"No, for real. Her hair ain't real, trust me on that."

"So, you're a hair expert now, too?" Dante folded his arms across his chest. Tyson was his boy, but sometimes the things that came out of his mouth were pure ignorance.

"My brother tells me all about these women that are so fine when you look at them, and then later, when you're alone with them, their nails come off, their eyes are contacts and their hair is from some horse's tail or some poor Indian girl who sold her hair to the temple to feed her family."

The table erupted into laughter, fueling Tyson on.

"Women do that." He nodded at each one of them while he talked, laying down the gospel like a preacher on Sunday morning. "I don't want me no fake shit." Tyson paused. "But from the look in your eyes—"

"What look?"

"You know what look I mean. Don't tell me you're a punk? I dare you to pull her ponytail. I bet you green money that thing comes right off in your hand."

"I ain't doing that, Man." Tyson's face burned. They were ogling him like they were looking at a parasite under a microscope. There was nothing worse than the boys thinking that he was soft. He wasn't, and they needed to know that. Before he had a chance to figure out his next move, Joyce walked past them again, this time, on the way to the trash can. Without thinking, Tyson jumped to his feet and strode toward her, his friends watching open-mouthed.

He reached her much faster than he'd anticipated, so fast that he had no time to think about what he was actually going to say.

"Hey," was all that came out of his mouth.

Joyce looked over her shoulder and gave a half-smile, half-laughing reply, but kept moving. Two girls giggled, too, as if someone had told a joke that no one had heard but the three of them. Dante felt anger bubbling up inside him. Who the hell did they think they were? She should be grateful he was even giving her the time of day.

His anger fueled new courage that surged through Dante's body. "Joyce?" he said. "Can I talk to you for a minute?" Their area of the room was quieter than before. It seemed as if everyone leaned in just a bit to be able to hear him better, to see if he was really as together as they thought he was, or if he was going to fall flat on his face, ignored and discarded by the new girl.

"I'm kind of busy." Joyce barely turned her head in his direction. She tossed a piece of paper in the trash can and pivoted, heading back in the direction of the table where she'd come from.

Dante reached out and grabbed for Joyce's arm, but missed. She sidestepped so gracefully, there was barely even time to notice that she'd dodged Dante's attempt. He grabbed again, this time catching the end of one of her ponytails. Dante's nose flared as he attempted to use it to pull Joyce toward him. Mouth open in surprise, she stumbled, but in the direction away from Dante.

Dante watched what happened next in slow motion. Joyce's tumble quickly morphed into a fall and then she was sliding across the lunchroom floor, face down. A deathly silence fell across the room. No one even breathed. Dante was frozen. Joyce grabbed her head, then slowly let out a long, slow, wail that reverberated throughout the lunchroom. The entire building quaked in sympathy.

A collective gasp ran through the room and Dante was momentarily confused. He looked at Joyce and stepped toward her to help her up. Face up, she scrambled backward away from him, crying loudly now. Dante stopped again, more confused. What just happened? Everyone, including his friends, was staring at him with shocked looks on their faces. Had he pushed her?

There was blood on Joyce's hands. Had she hit her head? Cut herself? Dante was unable to process what he was seeing. It didn't make sense. He looked down again and suddenly realized why Joyce had such a terrified look on her face, and everyone in the room seemed to notice it at the same time. The room erupted into noise. Dante stared at his hands in disbelief. He was holding what had been Joyce's braid, the one that was just attached to her head a moment ago. And he was pretty sure it was not a fake one.

Joyce's hair had been real. Dante couldn't think as he stared down at the tips of his shoes resting on the circular rug in the principal's office. Principal Gittens stood on the other side of his desk, staring at him and Joyce. She sat in the other chair, holding an ice pack to her head, whimpering every few seconds. Dante felt horrible. There was no way she would ever give him the time of day now.

"I'm trying to decide if we need to call your parents, Dante." Mr. Gittens checked the lock at least twice in the time it took him to complete that sentence.

Dante shook his head.

"I want my mother." Joyce's voice was filled with venom. Dante edged as far away from her in his seat as he could. "What if my hair doesn't grow back?"

"I think that is a bit of an overreaction, Joyce. Of course it will grow back." The principal glared in Dante's direction. "We don't want to make too big a deal out of this. I'm sure that Dante didn't mean to pull your hair out. Isn't that right, Dante?" His voice was stern.

Dante shook his head. Mr. Gittens was right. He hadn't meant for any of this to happen and had no idea how things had taken the turn they had. And he was also right about the other part; it really wasn't a big deal. *Joyce should have kept her mouth shut*, he thought. Defiance boiled up in him. If they called his mother, Joyce would regret it, he'd make sure of that. Dante sat back in his seat for the first time since he'd come into the office. Mr. Gittens's words had managed to make him feel better, a lot better.

The principal continued. "Joyce, I'm going to call your mother and let her know what happened. But I assure you that this is nothing more than a young man that was trying to get your attention." He feigned a smile. "And you have to feel good about that, right? Young ladies such as yourself always like it when they get attention. Isn't that right?"

Joyce frowned, but said nothing. A confused look came over her face as if she was no longer sure if her feelings were hurt or not.

The principal turned to him. "And Dante, this won't happen

again, am I right? I have your word?"

Dante hesitated a moment, then nodded. "No, sir, It won't. I didn't mean anything by it."

Joyce's shoulders dropped some and Mr. Gittens seemed satisfied. Dante felt instantly better. He knew he could have been in more trouble, and was glad that the whole thing was over with. "Can we go back to class now?"

Mr. Gittens paused and looked first at Joyce, then at Dante. He wrote something on his pad as the two looked on, waiting, then closed his portfolio with a thud. "Like I said, I don't want to see either of you in here again, you understand? Joyce, if you'd just talked to the young man, we could prevent things like this. Let's not mention this anymore. You both can go."

Joyce stood up, practically sliding out of the room, her head held low, walking as if she'd been scolded Dante rose, brushed off his jeans, and let out the breath he'd been holding for the past twenty minutes. He turned to leave, but the principal stopped him.

"Dante?"

"Yes, sir?"

"You are going to have to be more careful, young man, more subtle. It sometimes takes young women awhile to figure out what they want. She'll come around. They always do."

Dante nodded, then he drew himself up tall, adopting the walk that he'd come to know well, the one that said he ran things. If he wasn't sure he did before, he was sure now.

CHAPTER ONE

Ten years later

Rumer held her breath as she walked across campus. She couldn't help it. Not breathing helped her to suck in her imaginary stomach, making her feel long and lean in her head even if she didn't look it. Unlike some of her friends, Rumer looked every bit of her sixteen years and not a day more. Her string bean body hadn't yet sprouted womanly hips or the butt that gave a Kardashian badunkadunk a run for its money. She couldn't twerk and her shirt barely swelled as it ran over her chest. There wasn't a week that passed where her mother didn't look her up and down and proclaim, "Girl, you don't even have to walk past Victoria's Secret, much less think about wearing any."

During the regular school year, people had looked right by her as she walked through the halls of her high school. No one wanted to hang out with or date the skinny girl with a perfect four-point-zero GPA, but Rumer had no desire to be overlooked any longer. She'd learned to use something the other girls in her high school hadn't. While they had been lounging around on the weekends, Rumer took modeling classes. She'd learned how to wear makeup the right way, hold her head up and walk in a way that said she had something extra. She might feel like a bundle of nerves inside, but no one on the campus of City U's summer program would ever know it.

After weeks of practicing in the mirror, she strode across the campus as if she belonged there, turning heads with a quickness and supposed confidence of someone many years older and more experienced. Rumer's skirt floated near the tops of her tanned thighs. She looked straight ahead and walked toward the Robotics building. Passersby would momentarily confuse the walkway for a catwalk as they stepped out of her way. She left them helpless, wrenching their next breath from their lips as she passed.

The extra preparation she took every morning wasn't wasted, either. Although Rumer and her friends were attending a summer program for gifted students at "The U" as the local university was affectionately called, regular students were there, too. There were lots of students who were trying to get a jump on college, just like Rumer, but the campus was full of students trying to finish their degrees faster. There were also the athletes, most notably for Rumer, the football players, who reported for practice every single summer day, right before her class started.

Butterflies fluttered in Rumer's stomach as she approached the track where a group of players were running laps, the same as they did every morning. She slowed down a little, appreciating the circumstances that put these beautiful people in her path. In her fantasy, a well-muscled athlete would fall madly in love with her, and they would live happily ever after. There was certainly more to this than chance. Rumer wanted to look, but she wanted to be seen, too.

She rubbed her fingers together to wipe away the sweat, walking taller as she imagined the runners checking her out.

Rumer was well aware that gawking at athletes was not what she had come for. She was a smart girl, and she embraced that, but she was human. Last school year, she had either skipped or gone to every dance alone, and she was tired of that, even though she was positive her reclusiveness had made her parents happy. Rumer wanted more, and this summer, she was determined to get it. It had taken a good two weeks to even get the courage to take the long way to class, and she only had four more weeks left.

Two days ago, she'd noticed a few people run just a little slower as she passed, and yesterday, one of the players had practically slammed into someone else watching her. She'd smiled, thinking that her hard work was finally paying off. Rumer imagined that her days of being overlooked were coming to an end. She searched the track to see if she could spot a familiar physique. One hotness stuck in her mind. He was tall with long, lean legs, and not too thick like some football players.

He'd been running shirtless, and her mother would say that she could wash her clothes on his abs. She would say that, sure, Rumer thought, but she didn't want her daughter to be the one doing the washing. If it were up to her mother, Rumer would never have any fun and there would be no dating until graduate school, unless, of course, she approved of his pedigree. A frown spread across her face as she thought about her mother's double standards. She was supposed to be smart, but not dateless. Attractive, but not slutty. If she had no date, it was due to some imaginary thing she'd done wrong.

Rumer was just about past the track and there was no sign of Mr. Hot Body. Disappointment swelled over her. Hope dissipated with each step her Roman cage sandals took past the field. She'd probably only imagined him looking, anyway. She sighed, thinking that perhaps it was not meant to be. Maybe she was supposed to just go back to school for her senior year, sit through her boring classes, get all A's just like before, and then get shipped off to Spelman or Duke or somewhere fancy her mother wanted her to go, without ever being kissed. Perhaps her adventure was meant to come later. It was almost time for class to start anyway.

What had she been thinking? A few classes might have taught her how to walk like an angel, but that didn't mean she was one. She was still an unattractive girl, a pig in lipstick that walked like a supermodel. Everything outside was just a costume, a façade. Underneath all this, she was still just plain old Rumer Simone, the girl with the crooked smile. A girl who had really bad skin and big feet, no social life, and a bad case of a boring life. Her face flushed hot with embarrassment for no good reason, and familiar feelings of inadequacy visited her again.

Rumer took a deep breath and tried to push off the feeling of being cornered. She could barely cut it in high school, so who was she to think she could compete with these college women? Basic. That was what they'd called her. Every cell in her body had wanted to leave that label behind this summer, but it wasn't to be.

"Excuse me, Miss," a voice barraged through her thoughts.

Rumer was already so far down the slide of self-pity she almost didn't hear anyone talking. She kept walking, now intent on getting to her class.

"Excuse me," the voice said again, this time adding, "Are you going to the Robotics building?"

Her head jerked up, surprise flashing on her face.

"I have a question."

Rumer gasped. It was *him*. He had a shirt on today, a nice, crisp white one. Instead of missing him, Rumer was somehow looking into the running guy's light brown eyes, close enough to smell him, close enough to feel the heat coming from his body, and certainly closer than she thought she might get.

"I was wondering if you would be able to help me?"

He was talking to her. Rumer opened her mouth to speak, but no words came out. Her head was filled with visions of his washboard abs and all of the bravado she'd felt earlier was now gone.

"You okay?" he asked.

"Oh. Yes. I'm fine. But, but, I'm not a regular student. I'm—"

"What? Are you an irregular one, then?" His eyes twinkled and they laughed, his comment enough to break the ice.

Rumer forced herself to relax. She took a deep breath and tried to pull herself together, remembering once again, to stand with confidence. She smiled. "Oh, a smart ass."

"Can we start over?" He extended his hand. "I'm Dante. I'm lost. I need to find the seminar taught by Professor Perkins. It's supposed to be in room 301, but it's not."

"Well, it's nice to meet you, Dante." Rumer continued walking in the direction of her classroom. "I can show you where that is." Her heart skipped a beat. "Are you joining us? It's kind of late in the semester. We end in another few weeks. The professor moved the class two weeks ago. He said he liked the other lab better."

"Not exactly." He paused. "I guess I should just follow you then. How do you like the class so far?"

"It's okay, I guess. Lots of interesting stuff." Rumer blushed as Dante fell into step beside her. "I would think you knew your way around."

"And why would you think that?" Dante asked.

"Because it seems to me that even athletes have to take at least one freshman science class."

"They probably do." Dante smiled, revealing a dimple. "But this building is brand new. It just opened at the end of last semester. These classes are the first to be held in it."

"Oh," Rumer said.

"Actually, parts of the building, the upper floors, aren't even done yet." Dante paused as they reached the building entrance. "And I was actually an undergraduate student at the West Campus, not here. Wait, how'd you know I was an athlete?"

"Well, um…" Rumer stammered. "I saw you?" There was way too much question in her voice.

"Saw me?"

"Yes, running. On the track."

Dante nodded, then paused as if thinking. "Yes, I do that every day. Almost every day, anyway." An awkward silence passed between them. Dante finally extended his hand. "Thanks. I need to find the office. Enjoy your class."

Rumer's cheeks blushed red as she shook his hand. She should say something, but she was at a loss for words once again. She tried to sink through the floor when she realized that she was holding onto Dante's hand harder than he was holding hers.

He smiled, silently forgiving her. She released her grip just as the bell sounded, then headed down the hall toward her class.

CHAPTER TWO

Being late to class still made Rumer feel like she was a high schooler. She skulked into the room, keeping her head down as if that would make her less visible, and hoped that no one would notice. Anxiety marched up her spine like a line of ants on a pilgrimage. She sighed and some of the tension left her body as she realized that the room was still buzzing with students talking to one another. Relieved, Rumer made a beeline for a seat in the back of the room, her usual favorite place to sit, and didn't look up until she was nearly at her intended target. She glanced at her one friend in the class, Jenna, and nodded at her raised eyebrows.

The professor had not yet arrived. Normally, he would be there waiting as the students came in, welcoming them with a nod or a smile. Rumer glanced around, noting that no one seemed concerned that he wasn't there yet The guy next to her had his nose buried in whatever was on his phone and he didn't bother to look up as she passed. Rumer couldn't recall his name. He hadn't ever been particularly friendly during the class, either. Instead of talking to anyone, he was the type that spent most of his time staring at the device in his hand or out the window. She interrupted him anyway, tapping her finger on his desk. "Where's Professor Perkins?" she asked.

He completely ignored her, with the exception of raising his shoulders in an indifferent shrug. Jenna made a crazy face and twisted her mouth. Rumer stifled a laugh. That girl had a way about her that made everything comedic.

"So, what's the rule in college?" Jenna spoke to no one in particular. "We wait fifteen minutes and then we leave?"

Everyone continued talking. Rumer sat back in her seat, and looked around the room. Jenna was two rows to her side, tapping her pen on her notebook. Rumer contemplated going over to talk to her, but no one else was really walking around the room like she wanted to do. Some talked, but most sat quietly, either reading their phones or just waiting. About half the class was summer program kids like she was, but Rumer still didn't want to stick out. Although she was fighting to reinvent herself, it was hard to change years of purposely trying to be a part of the cool crowd.

It was a bright, sunshiny, beautiful day, and she was restless. If they could be outside an hour earlier, Rumer wanted to get to it. In Seattle, it didn't make sense to waste a beautiful day. That was one of the things about summer school that left her feeling confused. She understood the need for it, in principal. But in reality, she just wanted to be outside, laying under a tree or doing something fun like normal people. Or like the *fun* people. Her mother wouldn't agree. Rumer sighed. No matter what she did, her mother's voice was always in her head.

"Normal people end up bagging groceries for a living. You have to stay focused. You don't have the pretty to marry well." Rumer got it, but deep down, she sort of felt like focus was a synonym for boring. Her mother's message was clear. She was neither normal nor attractive, so she had to be smart, so here she was in summer school instead of outside enjoying the sun.

The clock moved at an impossibly slow pace. Rumer found herself holding her breath. Five minutes felt like an eternity. Just then, Dante walked into the classroom. Rumer frowned, then smiled. They were halfway done, but he would absolutely make the rest of the semester go faster if he'd transferred in. He looked at her and smiled, revealing a dimple on one cheek. It was so deep that Rumer immediately imagined sticking her tongue in it. Her breathing stopped for one second and she blushed.

Panic spread through Rumer, then she clenched her fist, digging her fingers into her palm. "Get it together, girl," she told herself. She was already letting her imagination run away from her. She pictured him sliding into one of the empty seats near her and her body felt hot.

"Hello, class." Dante's next words doused the fire that was already starting to burn and Rumer's mouth dropped open. He walked to the teacher's desk at the front of the room, putting his well-worn brown satchel on the desk. Rumer hadn't noticed that earlier.

"I'm so sorry I'm late," he said. "I had to run to the admin office to get the syllabus and instructions that Professor Perkins left me."

"Where is he?" someone called out. Rumer's eyes were wide as they remained locked on Dante. Her stomach churned. What was happening?

"He's not here," Dante answered. "In fact, he won't be here for the rest of the month. Unfortunately, Professor Perkins had a family emergency that took him out of the country for the next few weeks, so, you get me to complete the semester."

His words echoed in her mind. We get him for the rest of the semester? She couldn't make any sense of what he was saying. Was he going to be the instructor now? That couldn't be!

Someone else called out, "And you are?" In her head, Rumer answered, "Hot!" There was no other way for her to answer that. She shook her head. He couldn't be her instructor. She'd seen him with his shirt off. Wasn't there some rule that said instructors had to be...smart looking? Dante looked like he'd walked out of a Polo ad. And he looked young.

Dante paused, smiling. "I'm Dante Peterson. I'm a fifth year senior, majoring in Computer Science. I'm also Dr. Perkins's teaching assistant. I've been grading all of your lovely papers." He smiled. "You're in good hands."

A murmur went through the class. If Rumer were standing, she would have fainted. Another student raised his hand. "So, you haven't graduated yet?"

A broad smile spread across Dante's face, revealing that dimple. "No, I'm a fifth year student. I'm in the B.S. to M.S.

program, which means I earn both a Bachelor's Degree and a Master's Degree in five years."

So, he was smart, too, Rumer thought. There was something about a smart man that made him even more attractive. Rumer was still confused, though. He was a graduate student, an athlete, and now her instructor? She'd been shamelessly flirting with him just a few minutes before. Why hadn't he said something? Her face flushed hot again. He was so damned good looking. If he was a senior, that meant he was old, much older than a regular college guy.

The room took on a more polite tone. Someone raised their hand, but didn't wait to be called on. "So, if you're a graduate student—"

"I'm about finished, and I spent most of last semester on an internship, working in a lab at The University of Washington Research Center."

"And playing football."

Dante chuckled. "That too. I'm on my last year of eligibility. This whole building wasn't here last time I had an actual class in the Robotics department." He paused, looking from face to face. "And I'm also a teaching fellow, so I either teach or assist in two classes per semester at different colleges in the area. I plan to transition a doctoral program in robotics, so lucky for you, this class is one of my favorites. I'm hoping to make the rest of it a lot more fun for most of you."

"Are you saying Professor Perkins isn't fun?" someone asked.

Dante smiled, revealing a dimple. "Of course not. But he's not me." Dante pulled a stack of papers out of his bag and divided them up, dropping some of them on the desk at the front of each row. "Everybody take one and pass them back. I know that about half of you are high school students exploring your options. So, Professor Perkins and I decided to spice things up a bit by incorporating some real life projects into the class. We're going to take a more experiential approach during the second half of the class and get you into the lab. This handout will outline the projects we'll be doing. One per week."

Dante was no longer that charming guy that had asked her for directions. Instead, he'd taken on a more authoritative tone and seemed less hot and more smart. Rumer didn't know whether to be intimidated, or excited. Her stomach churned. She was a little of both. Dante continued talking, explaining how the rest of the semester would work. If *any* of the other students had doubts about him being legit or not, he made sure those doubts went out the window over the next fifteen minutes.

The hour went by quickly. Dante dove right in, and Rumer had difficulty being her normal, attentive self. Her mind kept wandering off as she alternated between shock and disbelief. In the short amount time she'd spent on a college campus, she'd gotten used to the idea that all professors looked a certain way. They were old and unattractive with round glasses and bellies to match. Guys who looked like Dante were not professors. They were athletes or actors or something like that. They weren't smart. Not usually, not like he sounded. Dante had kicked all of her preconceived notions about college out of the window.

She barely moved when the class ended. Her head was in a fog as she went through the motions of getting herself together. The students milled out of the classroom and Jenna appeared beside her desk. "You coming or what?"

Rumer nodded.

Jenna lowered her voice, turning her back to the front of the room. "Girl, tell me that is not the guy we were talking about the other morning?"

Rumer glared at her. Did Jenna have to be so obvious? Dante probably had no doubt that they were discussing him. "Let's talk about it later." They started toward the door. Rumer blushed again as she realized she would have to walk past him. All of the confidence she had earlier was now gone, replaced by embarrassment. Jenna chattered on uselessly.

"Rumer. Can I speak with you for a minute?" Dante's voice interrupted her thoughts.

Rumer and Jenna stopped in their tracks. Shock spread across both their faces.

"You can have her back in just a second," Dante said to Jenna, dismissing her. "This will only take a few minutes."

Jenna smiled, but raised her eyebrows as if to ask a question.

Dante cocked his head to the side. His smile was crooked. Her stomach jumped again. Was that a twinkle in his eye? His gaze was way too friendly for a professor.

Dante seemed to sense her hesitation. "I won't bite," he said.

Rumer's mouth went dry. "S-s-sure," she stammered, "Professor—"

"Just Dante."

Jenna looked from Rumer to Dante with a question on her face. Her eyes narrowed. "I'll meet you out front."

Rumer nodded, her heartbeat pounding in her ears. They waited as Jenna left, silent until the door closed behind her.

Dante's voice punctuated Rumer's surprise. "I should have put two and two together. I didn't realize you were *that* Rumer when we were talking earlier."

Did she like the way that sounded? "What Rumer is that?"

Dante waved a graded paper in the air. "I've been grading your essays, remember? I know from reading them that you are really interested in robotics." He paused. "That being said, I think I have an opportunity you'll really find intriguing."

Rumer's thoughts were all over the place. *He had an opportunity?* She blushed. There were of all sorts of things he could offer her that she might be interested in. She gave herself a mental slap and tried to pull her mind out of the gutter.

Dante cleared his throat. "That is, if you're interested in getting some extra college credit. It will make your college applications much stronger."

All thoughts of Dante's hotness left her brain. The mention of college stirred a remembrance of the reason why she'd come to the summer program in the first place, and she was suddenly embarrassed by where her thoughts had been going. Rumer really *was*

28

interested in Robotics. Her parents had been so proud when she was offered the opportunity to attend this summer program free of charge, and she was interested in anything that could help her get as far away from home for college as she could.

"I'm interested. Very interested, actually."

"I thought so. You seemed passionate about that in the essay you wrote during the first week of class. I know students think that we don't read the answer to the 'why are you here' question, but we really do." Dante was beaming now. He continued. "We are working on a mobility project in the lab, in conjunction with the medical lab. I'm sure you can be a fly on the wall for a bit." His passion for his work was obvious, and with that on his face, he somehow looked more professor-like to Rumer.

Her eyes widened. "Wow." She was unsure of what she should say next. "A special project?" Many students would kill for an opportunity like this, especially ones that were working on getting into a good school.

"I'll take that as a yes," Dante said. "I'll email you the details and where to be. You'll have to come to my lab in the evenings. Will that be a problem?"

Rumer could barely muster a nod. She might have to explain it to her mother some, but this was college, and unlike high school, classes and opportunities happened all hours of the day.

"I'll find a way to make it work." Rumer was almost not distracted by Dante's dimple this time. He really did look smarter to her now.

"You okay?"

"Oh, yes. Sorry." Rumer was so lost in the possibilities, she didn't realize that he'd stopped talking and she was just standing there, daydreaming.

"I'm sure your friend is waiting," Dante said. "Just look for my email tonight, then." Rumer wanted to pinch herself. She couldn't believe that she was going to get to work on a special project, and her mother would be so happy about the possibility of college credit. This was an amazing opportunity, there was no doubt about that, one that got even more amazing when she factored in the opportunity to work with Dante. He was most certainly too old, but that didn't matter. There was nothing wrong with injecting a little fantasy into school.

Chapter Three

"So, let me get this straight…" Jenna and Rumer were supposed to be studying in the small dorm room they shared, but instead, Rumer was being grilled. "That guy, the one we have been watching, is a teacher's assistant? A grad student?"

"He might as well be." Rumer nodded. "He's a fifth year student. I know, I'm disappointed, too."

"But he's so hot."

"--Understatement." She held up her hand, signaling Jenna to stop talking. Rumer really didn't want to talk about Dante anymore. She and Jenna had been over the same thing countless times since the day before, and she was working on removing the memory of Dante's hotness from her brain. "I thought he was an athlete here working out for the summer or something."

Jenna nodded. "We both did." She pouted. "What a waste. He's so fine. I could barely concentrate while he was talking."

Rumer sighed, sheepishly locking onto Jenna's eyes. "I know, right?" They both laughed. It was funny now. They'd spent almost a whole week planning to run into Dante or one of his fellow runners. None of that mattered anymore.

"How are we supposed to learn anything in that class now?" Jenna fidgeted, bouncing her pen off the desk.

"Girl, tell it. Plus, now he's chosen me to work on some project in his lab."

"Ooo. He's *chosen* you." Jenna stopped short. "What? Is that what the 'Miss Jackson, can I talk with you for a minute?' was about?

Rumer nodded. "It's good, though. It actually looks like it's going to be interesting." She turned back toward her computer. "I really need to get all of this work done today, though. I don't know how you finished it already."

Jenna cleared her throat. "I didn't, not exactly."

"What are you saying? It's due day after tomorrow." Although theirs was a program just for the summer, they were treated like everyone else on campus. "We have to get it in."

"I'll get it done. I always do."

The girls flopped down on the floor near their books, ready to buckle down on their assignment. They'd established a routine; power through all of the hard stuff as soon as they got home and that would leave the rest of the afternoon and evening for more fun summer things, like movies and malls and whatever else they could get into.

Jenna flipped open her Robotics book and Rumer leaned back, flipping through her notes. Her phone flashed and they both jumped. "I can't get used to that," Jenna said. They both laughed a bit. Jenna's phone flashed every time she got a notification. "It's like lightning is in the room with you."

"It's better than vibrating everything in the room with your phone on silent. I hate that. If you can hear it buzz, then that isn't silent." Rumer grabbed her phone and unlocked it, moving quickly to her text messages. She scrolled through the list, frowning. "I don't know who this is from."

"Huh? What do you mean?" She was distracted as she tried find the assignment she was looking for. "Just read it. Better yet, why don't you put it over on the other side of the room so we can actually get some work done?"

Rumer waved her off as she tapped the new message. Since when was Jenna so dedicated to school? Half of the reason she wanted to be there was because she had nothing else to do. Rumer read the text out loud. "Are you free tonight?"

"You know I have stuff to do," Jenna answered.

"Not you. That's what this message says." She paused, a perplexed look on her face. "But I have no idea who this is. I don't recognize this number at all."

"So ask, Rocket Scientist. Just hurry up and figure it out, so we can get back to business. I have a ton of other things I can do once we finish here. Things that are a lot more fun. And then tell them you'll be hanging with me."

Rumer took a deep breath, but before she could fire off a response, another message came in.

Hey, this is Dante, by the way. There is a party on campus and I was wondering if you'd like to go. No big deal, just a few folks getting together.

Rumer leaned back to steady herself. She was confused, a fight going on in her brain. Dante was hot. He was her TA. He was inviting her to a party. It didn't sound like this party had anything at all to do with his research. Or was he trying to get to know her?

Jenna was not so patient as she looked on. "Well? Who is it? Can we get to the assignment now?"

Rumer struggled for words. "Um, it's from Dante."

Jenna scowled. "Are you guys gonna start working already? I know it's a big deal, but this lab thing doesn't sound like any fun, especially if you are going to spend the rest of the summer holed up doing robotics research. You know that's not normal, right? I mean, who wants to do that?"

Rumer tried her best to hold back her smile. "Nope, no lab. You're not going to believe this, but he's inviting me to a party."

"Who is the he you mean?"

Rumer cocked her head to the side, raising her eyebrows. Did she have to spell it out?

Jenna's mouth dropped open, and then she squeaked. "Like, a college party? Does he know how old you are?"

"I think so." A moment of silence passed between them, then they both jumped up and danced a few steps as if the dorm room were a football end zone.

"Well? Are you going to go?"

Rumer didn't hesitate. "Absolutely."

They high-fived. It had taken awhile, but it seemed like the summer had finally begun.

Rumer squealed with delight, firing off her response right

away.

I'll be there. Send me the address.

That's what's up.

"So, who is this that you're inviting to our soiree?"

Dante licked his fingers and then ran them along the length of his sideburns. *I'm gonna need to be edged up soon*, he thought. "Don't you worry. It's just one of my students."

Tyrone smiled, making air quotes with his fingers as he spoke. "Just one of your students, huh? Since when have you invited someone from one of your classes to hang out with us?"

"Chill, man. I'm not inviting her to hang. I just want to make her more comfortable. You know, get her introduced to our project. You know how I do." He played with the razor in his hand, staring into the mirror. He liked his face to be perfect.

"Yes, I do know how you do. That's what I'm worried about. You're like Kryptonite to women or something. You're all nice to them and then the next thing we know, they're putty in your hands. After that, they're heartbroken and crazy and their friends are talking them off the ledge."

A small laugh escaped his lips. "Don't hate. I just give them what they want, just like when we were kids."

Tyrone paused and looked hard at his friend. "Exactly. It's not like you ask them what they want. You guess."

"No, my friend. You are mistaken." A sly smile spread across

Dante's face. "I *intuit* it."

CHAPTER FOUR

Jenna pruned in front of the full-length mirror beside Rumer. She smoothed her hands over her body-con dress and pursed her lips. "Thanks for inviting me to this party. Did they say you could do that? Bring someone?"

"I didn't ask." Rumer shrugged. "And you're not someone. You're my girl. We're a package deal. Besides, what are they going to do? Ask me to leave? Not let me in? Either way, that would tell me some valuable information." She paused, taking in her reflection. "And I kinda need you for backup. I still have no idea why Dante is inviting me here." As much as she tried to act as if she was all as a college student, there was a part of her that kept being reminded that she was really just a high school kid, and no amount of new clothing could keep her from feeling like an imposter or like she didn't belong. She'd felt like an outsider for so long that it was a hard feeling to shake.

"I do." Jenna answered. "As smart as you are, you can't figure it out? C'mon now. He's got the hots for you, girl. He'd be stupid not to."

"Let's not jump to any conclusions, okay?" Rumer applied her lipstick, and looked calm on the outside, but the truth was that butterflies tickled her stomach. She felt like she was in middle school and had a crush she didn't know what to do with. Her head was telling her it was probably nothing, but her heart so wanted what Jenna was saying to be true. Dante might be a few years older, but so what? What was it that Aaliyah sang in that song her mother played over and over? Age ain't nothing but a number, right? She cocked her head to the side, admiring her handiwork. "Is it weird that he's a teacher?"

"It's not like he's really a professor. He's a student. Just like us," Jenna said. The voice in the back of her head was trying hard to find ways to make sense of everything. She was flattered, but no one had really shown much interest in her before, especially not someone older.

There was a certain excitement to getting dressed up to go to a college party. Both Jenna and Rumer felt as if they were taking more steps toward adulthood with each step of the dressing process. "Did you tell your mother what we were doing?" Jenna suddenly asked.

"Did you tell yours?" Rumer frowned. "Why in the world would I do that? So she could tell me not to go? I might not even answer if she calls." Although she'd said it, Rumer didn't even believe that herself. She knew that if she didn't answer her mother's calls or texts too many times, it would be nothing for her to turn off her data or even her phone until she did.

"Girl, please, if I did that, my mother would be livid."

Rumer nodded. Her mother was absolutely strict about the

phone. "Mine always says that she gives me a phone so she can contact me when she wants to, so let's just hope she doesn't call. I'll tell her I was asleep." Rumer sat on her bed and grabbed her shoes. They were much higher than what she was used to, but she had no plans on running anywhere. "More than likely, she'll text instead of call anyway. And you can't hear party noise with a text message, so we're good."

If they were at home, they'd have to tell their mothers where they were going, maybe even ask permission, and if they were going, there is no way either one would have gotten out of the house in the outfits they were wearing. Living in the dorms wasn't glamorous, but it presented a whole other level of freedom that both girls were getting used to quickly. Rumer's mother wouldn't have agreed to even buying the dress she had on, either. She could hear her mother now, telling her that the dress was appropriate for nothing. It fit Rumer like it was body paint instead of fabric and was just long enough to cover her backside. She'd told her mother that this was the style over and over again. "*Style* is overrated," she'd say. "Real style endures and there is nothing enduring about that little piece of cloth. It won't last two washes, so you don't need to bother wearing it." If it were up to her mother, she'd be walking around looking like she'd run away to join the Amish or something. Rumer shook off the thoughts of her disapproving paternal unit. Since they were away, none of that applied.

CHAPTER FIVE

The party wasn't hard to find. It was actually off-campus, but only about three blocks, so it was an easy walk. They'd looked up the location on the phone, and then carefully plotted when they should leave. Rumer and Jenna didn't want to arrive too early; that would be awkward, and too late would be weird.

"The trick is to arrive at exactly the right time," Rumer said.

"And what makes the time right?"

"We don't want to be the first ones there. People should see us when we arrive. We'll be able to maximize exposure. Most eyes on us when we walk in, get it?" The girls nodded together as Rumer's logic came together.

"And you learned this from—"

"Girl, stop. I just know." She applied her lipstick without blinking. "I read it in a magazine. That's how the famous people do it. You think Beyoncé arrives right on time when she goes out? I think not."

Jenna rolled her eyes, shaking her head at her friend's wisdom. "And if it's in a magazine or on the Internet, it must be true." She paused. "Sometimes, you're just too trusting. Not to mention that Beyoncé is most certainly a genius."

"Just appreciate that I do all of this research. It could save us some embarrassment," Rumer said.

"Whatever, girl." Jenna waved her hand dismissively. "You would be a rocket scientist for real if you focused this energy on things that really mattered."

"You sound like an old woman."

"Maybe. But old women get to be old and wise for a reason." They were dressed quickly, and they fidgeted in the lobby of the dorm while they waited for the right time. They checked and rechecked their outfits in the big mirror that hung there until, finally, the time they had agreed on arrived. They didn't even have to talk, both girls stood up, paused, and then headed for the door to make the short walk over to the party.

Although the path was well lit by streetlamps, both Jenna and Rumer wrapped their arms around their bodies, pulling their flimsy sweaters tight around themselves. They listened hard, acutely aware of the night around them. It was pretty cool for summer, but temperatures in Seattle never got that hot anyway. Neither one of them said anything as they walked. Rumer was tense. The anticipation from wondering how the party was going to be and fantasizing about what she was going to say to Dante left her words lost in the dream world inside her head. Jenna was cold and she hummed to herself as they walked, concentrating on avoiding cracks in the sidewalk. At any moment, she expected her shoes to betray her and throw her down into the tiniest of holes.

The well-lit street didn't take away from the brightness in front of the house, which was dead center in the middle of campus. Light from two streetlamps flooded the small front yard, revealing that the place was run down and in need of paint. The black house numbers had, at one point, been attached to a white doorjamb, but now the second number was missing and the last hanging by a thread. Rumer and Jenna knew it was the right house because the missing number had left a dirt outline in its place.

An old-fashioned porch bordering the house had seen better days and was in need of repair in several places. Remnants of a dark grey paint were left behind, now cracked and peeling in many places. The worn boards bowed downward, having yielded to many years of college-aged residents traipsing across it as they came and went. Altogether, the building looked left over from another era.

A large crowd spilled from the house into the yard. Even if they didn't have the address, it was easy to recognize the party. There were people sprawled all over the porch and the thin lawn, and a few perched in the large tree that reigned over the front yard. Music and people poured from the building, vibrating the street.

The girls hesitated, then made their way to the front door, both now doubting their decision to arrive when most eyes could be on them. Instead of feeling seen, they felt scrutinized. Neither turned their heads, instead keeping their eyes trained on the front door, which was agape. The light from within kept them from seeing inside from where they stood. They walked past people holding red cups and Rumer was acutely aware of the heads that turned in their direction, some staring them down so hard she felt sure they could see through the thin material of her body conscious dress. Rumer knew it was in her head, but she'd never felt more naked in her life.

"Maybe we shouldn't have come," Rumer whispered.

Jenna held herself tighter. "It'll be fine," she answered, her words hollow. She looked down to avoid making eye contact with anyone. They both held themselves tighter, sure that everyone could see that they were really high school girls playing dress up. For a split second, Rumer felt like a fraud. The small yard stretched out forever like a ribbon as they crossed it. While they walked the short distance, Rumer had flashbacks of all of her years in high school. Feeling out of place was a feeling she was quite familiar with.

Although people looked, no one stopped them. Rumer hesitated at the door and Jenna almost ran into her. She nudged her gently, pushing her across the threshold. They both practically tumbled into the packed room.

The music wrapped itself around them and dampened their ears. Rumer's eyes widened. As soon as they were through the door, they were thrust into the middle of a gyrating crowd. The room itself smelled heavily of sweet smoke, a smell they both recognized. They exchanged glances, but both tried their best to keep their faces as straight as possible. Rumer didn't want to act as if anything was a big deal. This was college, after all.

A very tan boy leaned against the wall and smiled at Jenna, holding out his hand to her. He gestured and offered her a bit of what he was smoking. She blushed, then stopped herself, shaking her head no. Although Marijuana was legal in Washington, she knew she still had to be twenty-one to smoke it. They'd probably get a contact high from just breathing in this place, and that was higher than she was willing to be. A breeze from a ceiling fan moved the air in the room, and the skin on the back of Rumer's neck prickled.

Rumer pushed her friend playfully in the arm, grinning. "What?"

"Not for me," Jenna answered. She kept her poker face. "He's a cutey and all, but I have no intention of catching a case for anyone. I have things to do and orange is not my color."

"I know that's right," Rumer agreed.

The girls continued into the dimly-lit room. As they got further in, their clothes began to glow.

"Black lights," Rumer whispered, hoping there was no lint on her that she wasn't able to see before. The furniture in the room had been draped in sheets, and they, like the clothing of the people in the room, gave off a ghostly glow. Rumer glanced down at her fingernails. The white tips of her French manicure emanated a slightly green essence. It was kind of freaky, but she liked it. Her pulse quickened. A surge of courage ran through her and her lips curled into a smile for the first time since she'd arrived. The light added to the excitement of things.

Rumer's heartbeat kept time with the music. She looked around, trying to catch her breath. Where was Dante? It was hard to tell who anyone was, but she squinted and tried to spot him anyway. The music was so loud it would be hard to talk to him, even if she did know what she was going to say.

"I thought your boo was supposed to be meeting you here?"

Jenna seemed to read her mind.

"Yeah, I thought he'd be at the door to meet us, but I never said he was my boo. He could have just invited me to be nice."

"Neither one of us believes that."

Rumer didn't reply, but Jenna was right. Or at least Rumer hoped she was. She knew that it was weird that Dante was her teaching assistant, but he was so fine, she didn't care. He wasn't *really* a professor, so it could work out, right?

The music changed to a more up-tempo song, one that Rumer recognized immediately. It was the hit of the season, played all over the radio, except it had a dance beat behind it. A roar flowed across the room, and people that had been standing and talking or sitting jumped to their feet and started dancing. One girl jumped on the small coffee table and swayed from side to side, her drink held in one hand, cigarette in the other. Rumer and Jenna looked at each other and made a face. "Drunk girl is not a good look," Jenna said.

Rumer raised her eyebrows in silent agreement. Drunk girl was definitely *not* a good look. Add smoking on top of that and you had a hot mess. Her mother would kill her if she even thought about doing anything like that, not that she wanted to. It just wasn't cute.

Jenna and Rumer shrunk back, letting themselves be moved to the side by the crowd instead of being surrounded by its growth. Their eyes widened. "Aren't you going to get in there, Rumer? You know you love to dance."

Rumer shook her head back and forth quickly as she took it all in. "I think I'll just watch."

Jenna made a face at her friend, but moved with her anyway. The girls backed out of what was now the center of the dance floor. Rumer moved her head from side to side to the music, trying to look like she belonged, instead of scared.

They almost reached the safety of the wall on the side of the room, but Rumer's retreat was stopped by someone's hands on her arms from behind. "Oh, sorry," she said, thinking she'd backed into someone.

"Don't be." Dante's voice was very close to her ear, so close, that chills ran through her. Rumer whirled around. "Oh—"

"I'm sorry I was late. I got tied up in the lab." He smiled, and Rumer felt her knees go weak. It should be a crime for someone to be that fine.

He leaned against a pole that divided the room, then flicked something off of Rumer's shoulder. "Oh, it's not a problem. We just got here anyway." All of the courage that Rumer had felt before she left her dorm room came rushing back. Her cheeks flushed. Here was this impossibly fine older guy, and he was paying attention to no one but her.

Suddenly, she felt as if she were being watched. Rumer looked over Dante's shoulder. She wasn't imagining it. There was a guy behind Dante, off to the side, and he was staring right at her. He made no effort to look away. Instead, he half-smiled, nodded and then raised his red cup in Rumer's direction. She blushed and nodded back, then looked away.

"Don't mind my boys." Dante tilted his head in the direction of the guy with the red cup. "We all came together. We run together. Go way back."

Rumer nodded, then looked over Dante's shoulder again. The boy that raised his cup to her was leaning over and talking in the other, shorter boy's ear. "Okay, I get that. Me and my friends run together, too," she said. "I want you to meet my friend, Jenna. Thanks for letting me bring her."

"What?" Dante said. "It's hard to hear over the music." His eyes scanned the room.

Rumer gestured to Jenna, who was now a bit apart from her on the edge of the crowd, but moving to the music as if she was having a good time. She half waved, but kept moving. Although she looked around like she wasn't paying attention, Rumer knew that Jenna would read her lips if the music wouldn't let her hear what she was saying.

As if she'd been waiting for her cue, Jenna was by her side almost faster than Rumer could blink. She didn't wait to be introduced. She stuck her hand out. " Hey, Dante, I'm Jenna. I'm in your class, too." A big grin spread across her face.

Rumer cringed and almost melted through the floor. Why in the world did Jenna have to be so goofy? Her mention of school brought Rumer back down off the cloud she was on, reminding her of the real reason she was there.

If Dante recognized Jenna, Rumer couldn't tell. He gave no indication that he'd met her before at all. He paused, ran his tongue over his bottom lip, then took Jenna's fingertips. "It's a pleasure to me you. Jenna, is it?"

A giggle escaped Jenna's lips. "It is. I mean, I am." She nodded, and he brought her hand to his lips and gently kissed it. Both girls were stunned. Their mouths dropped open in surprise.

Who does that? Rumer thought. *That was some movie star mess right there.* Confused, Rumer's heart fluttered. It took a minute for the girls to recover.

"Okay, well, um. That's nice." Rumer didn't know what else to say. Hand kissing was kind of awkward anyway, and almost weird with all of these people around. And Dante didn't kiss her hand, he'd kissed Jenna's. She wasn't sure how to feel about that. She fidgeted a little. If she didn't know better, Rumer might think what she was feeling was jealously. She pushed that thought away. Dante was her instructor and nothing more. There was not a lotto be jealous of when you broke it down.

"You two are so lovely," Dante said.

Rumer frowned. *Lovely? What did that mean?*

"I'm really glad you could make it. I think it's a great way for us to get to know each other. Especially if we are going to work together."

Rumer felt deflated. There it was. So his invitation *was* about work, after all. She tried not to look as disappointed as she felt. She'd jumped to crazy conclusions because of one text message. How could she have been so stupid? Maybe her mother was right. Maybe her head really was always in the clouds. It looked like summer wasn't going to be as much fun as she'd thought.

"Why don't you guys get yourselves something to drink?" Dante said. "The sodas are over there." He pointed toward the back of the house.

The girls looked in that direction, but didn't move. Rumer fought back tears. Were they being pointed toward the kiddie table? Is this what Dante really thought of her? That she was nothing but a kid?

"I have to go and talk to some people, and I'll catch up with you later. Maybe we can talk a bit about the lab setup and what we are working on. What do you think, Rumer?"

He didn't wait for an answer, and all Rumer could do was nod. She was so confused.

"Okay. I'm really glad you could make it." Dante held onto each of Rumer's shoulders, practically holding her in place while looking at her hard. He had a partial grin on his face. Or maybe it was a smirk. Rumer couldn't tell which.

She squirmed. She felt dismissed, and was nothing but relieved when he finally let her go. Dante strode off toward the back of the house, leaving the girls where they stood. Rumer blinked back tears.

"That was weird." Jenna finally broke the silence.

"It was." Rumer paused. "I kinda want to go home."

"Just say the word and we're out."

"The Word." Rumer was sure that Jenna would ask questions later, but for now, she didn't want to talk. She just wanted to get home and curl up in the hard dorm room bed and figure out why she had gone through all that effort...for nothing.

CHAPTER SIX

There was less noise and more light in the old kitchen at the back of the community house. Dante leaned against the sink and drained the beer can he held, then crushed it with one hand.

"Oh, Mr. Strong Man," Tyrone said, then punched him playfully on the shoulder. "Ow. That hurt," he mocked. He shook out his hand like his light blow had caused some damage to his own hand.

"Maybe if you concentrated on working out half as much as you do those lame-ass jokes, you wouldn't injure yourself by touching me."

The four guys in the room laughed easily together. This was a familiar sight. During each of these parties, Dante and his friends all gravitated to the small, aged kitchen at the back of the house. It had become somewhat of a ritual for them. This was how they debriefed, standing together at the rear of the house as if it were their own version of Pride Rock.

The house had been in the middle of town before the university had grown so big and had enveloped it, gobbling it up and everything else in its path. A developer wanted to tear it down, but to honor the wishes of the original owner, the house had instead been preserved and absorbed into the university. Over the years, the proud home had served many purposes ranging from office to satellite classroom, and had finally been turned into a gathering spot for students. Most students had attended a social event or two during their time at the school. This building, and really the kitchen, was the center of student after-hours events and all of the students were very familiar with it, and many actually preferred it to some of the newer buildings on campus. The small house leaned to the side and the floorboards creaked, but to many of the students, it felt most like home.

Roderick leaned back against the wall. "So what's up with that young hottie you were talking to?"

Dante shrugged, not wanting to answer.

"Don't give me that, man. You think I don't know what time it is?"

Before he could answer, they were interrupted by three girls. "Hey Dante," they chirped in unison and their presence immediately filled the kitchen with noise. They all wore a variant of the same outfit, body-conscious dresses that just covered their behinds, paired with clunky heels that made their legs appear ten miles long. "You guys gonna hide in here all night?"

One of the girls reached out and ran her hand over Dante's firm midsection. "You're looking good. What are you up to these days?"

The other guys moved back and let Dante be the center of attention. They were used to it. "Same stuff. Classes. Teaching. You know how it is." He squirmed, but couldn't move away. He was stuck between the newcomer and the kitchen sink.

"Do we?" she purred. "Why don't you come tell me how it is? In my ear." She paused, looking around the room. "Like alone."

Dante smiled warmly. "Ranisha, I'm going to have to catch up with you a little later. I'm talking to my boys right now. We have some things to discuss."

Ranisha looked around the room nervously, a scowl on her quickly reddening face. "Really? You'd rather do that then hang out with me? I really need to talk to you."

"It's not like that, woman." Dante put his arm around her waist and pulled her to him. "It's just that I know once I get with you, I'm done for the night. I'd want to give you all of my time. You deserve that. I need to handle some business first. Why don't you go on out there and enjoy yourself?" Dante turned on the charm. "I promise I will catch up with you soon." He kissed her on the forehead.

Everyone watched the show in silence. Ranisha pouted. "You have my number? Just in case? Because you've told me that same thing before. I'm beginning to think you really don't like me at all, Dante."

"You know what? Let's put it in my phone, just in case." He handed the girl his phone and they waited while she entered her number. Dante winked at his friends, over her shoulder. He wanted to be sure they saw how he handled his business.

Ranisha opened the camera and took a selfie and added it to her listing. "This way, you'll know exactly what you're getting."

"Oh, I know what I'm getting." He locked his eyes on hers. "I'll holler."

Ranisha nodded, but took the way out that Dante had given her. Roderick cleared his through and the room seemed to pause as they waited.

"Okay then." A seductive smile came across Ranisha's face. "If you promise." She backed away from Dante. Her friends turned to leave.

"I do. I'll get with you later." Dante smiled hard, his eyes twinkling like he was on *America's Next Top Model*. He raised his eyebrows slightly, then lowered them, knowing that this worked almost every time. Ranisha would be dazzled by his dimples and his charm, in that order. He didn't want to hurt her feelings, especially in front of everyone.

They all waited as Ranisha and her crew exited the room, but no one said anything until they disappeared through the door. As soon as Ranisha was no longer visible, the kitchen erupted into laughter.

Dante tried to keep a straight face, but his grins quickly gave way to laughs.

"Man, you are too smooth," Roderick said. "I ain't never seen anyone deal with a thirsty chick like you. What's wrong with her? Not your type?"

"Been there, done that."

"Oh, I see, It's like that? Hit it once—"

"Once? I hit that four times. But you know how it is, once you get a little bit of Dante in your system, you can't do without."

Roderick stopped laughing. "Is that so? So, you're crack now? Folks get addicted?"

"Crack is a poor man's drug. I'm the good stuff. Like heroin or cocaine." He ran his hand on his stomach, the same place Ranisha had touched.

"What you are is stupid. There was nothing wrong with that woman. She was a fine sister."

Dante crossed his arms, resting his chin between two fingers. "She was fine, but she was old news. I want to move on to newer, fresher things."

Roderick grinned. "Newer, huh? You got it like that? You just throw away all the fine sisters." The guys laughed as Roderick looked around the small room for confirmation. "Like younger? Like those two young things you were talking to? You trying to catch a case, my friend?"

The room roared with laughter again.

"You need to mind your business." Dante tried his best to stifle a grin.

"They *were* cute, but they looked kind of young."

"They were both older than seventeen." Dante paused.

"Maybe." Roderick nodded. "True. But just because they're young doesn't mean they're yours for the picking. That just seems like too much work. A more mature woman would be easier to deal with."

"Who said *I* did the picking? You know that women are really the ones in control. Deep down, they have desires and it is our job to uncover and guide them through. I already know that one of them wants me." He licked his lips.

"Who taught you this shit?"

"A better question is why don't you know it?" Now, they all laughed with Dante. "Trust me, it's all good. Young lady might be a little young, but she knows a good thing when she sees it."

"You sure about that?" Tyrone spoke up, annoyance dancing around his face.

"Of course, I am. They all want it. Just watch, I guarantee I'll have Rumer on my arm by the end of the week. By next month, she'll be writing her first name and my last in her diary. Trust and take notes."

"Next month? That fast, huh? You have skills."

"I was trying to leave room for the unexpected. I really think it will be next week. Yeah, she'll be wrapped around my little finger by then."

Ranisha stopped smiling as soon as she and her entourage step out of the kitchen. She clenched her fists and reopened them repeatedly, but kept walking and made sure her face appeared relaxed. None of the losers behind her needed to see her frustration.

"Girl, I think he blew you off. So much for feeling you?"

" He is. Dante is. He's just trying to play things off in front of his boys." She faked a laugh. "I get it, though, he doesn't want them all up in our business. I can appreciate that." Ranisha didn't think any of her friends bought her story, but she had no intention of letting them know that. She took a deep breath. Instead of discussing Dante further, she bopped her head to the beat that dominated the room. She joined in with the other party folk, dancing but not quite dancing, and her friends did, too. Before she knew it, Dante was pushed to the back of her mind, and she and her girls were jamming to Kendrick Lamar. In her head, he was talking directly to her. She was so lost in the music, Ranisha was taken completely by surprise when she felt a pair of hands on her waist from behind.

She swung around, ready to fight, but relaxed quickly when she saw who it was. Dante placed his face in her neck from behind, and she struggled to hold back a grin. She was right. He had been just keeping stuff from his friends.

"I'll get with you later, okay, girl?" his voice rumbled through her body.

Ranisha didn't have time to answer. As fast as he'd touched her so intimately, Dante was past her and gone. She was speechless as she watched Dante stride through an opening in the door and out the front of the house. The warm feeling that had rushed over her faded to a chill. She shivered as if someone had just snatched a warm blanket off of her. How did he do that? In just a few seconds, Ranisha's emotions had run the gamut from lust to loathing, all directed at the same person.

She fumed as her girls looked on, confused. All of the mixed messages left her not understanding how Dante could treat her the way he had. He claimed he liked her and his words kept promising that they'd get together again, but his actions made Ranisha not so sure. She glared at her friends, but no one dared say anything.

Before she knew what was happening, Ranisha was headed toward the front door, propelled forward by her rage. The other girls exchanged glances and then fell into formation behind Ranisha, who followed Dante at a respectable distance, not caring that an entourage trailed behind her like a dover of ducks. She didn't know what she was going to do when she caught up to him, but she could worry about that later. Right now, she refused to be thrown away like a used tissue. Again.

CHAPTER SEVEN

Rumer and Jenna were silent as they walked back to the dorm room, both wrapping their arms around their bodies. It felt cooler now than it had earlier, and the light evening breeze left both the girls with a chill. They walked away from the party and the bass of the music faded with each step. By the time they reached the corner, except for the occasional car, the click of their heels on the pavement was the only sound either heard.

Rumer was crushed as she thought about the evening, though she wasn't sure why. Nothing about the party or Dante had turned out as she had imagined it would. He was her instructor, but the party invitation had been anything but instructor-like. She'd thought he was into her, but that didn't seem to be the case at all. A text invitation. Who does that for a business meeting? What else could she had possibly thought he'd meant when he invited her? She bit her lip as she ran through all of the possibilities in her head, but in the end, she still came out feeling like an idiot.

In person, all of the signals he'd given her were mixed, too. She was even more confused than she'd been when he'd asked her to come. It was a shame. She'd wasted all of that time getting dressed up, and making sure her makeup and hair were perfect, for nothing. If she'd known she was being asked out for a meet and greet instead of the romantic encounter she'd pictured in her mind, she could have stayed in her jeans and not pushed her feet into these tortuous shoes that had a fifteen-minute shelf life. Not to mention, she'd wasted valuable studying hours. If he'd been truthful with her, she might have skipped the party altogether. Things like this weren't really her scene anyway. On one hand, she felt like Dante wanted more, but that was not what his actions were saying. She just couldn't make any sense of it.

"Someone is calling you, girl," Jenna's voice jarred her back to the present.

"What? I don't think so. My phone isn't ringing."

Jenna grabbed her arm, stopping her in her tracks. "No, for real, listen."

Almost as soon as Jenna uttered the words, Rumer did indeed hear someone calling her. "Rumer," they yelled, "wait up!" Butterflies tickled her stomach as she squinted into the darkness behind her. If she didn't know any better, she'd be positive that Dante was yelling her name down the street. Her heartrate jumped back up again. No one would do *that* for a business meeting.

Jenna's disapproval poured out of her body before she even spoke. "I wouldn't even talk to him if I were you. He basically blew you off not ten minutes ago. Let's go." She grabbed her friend's arm to lead her toward the dorm.

Rumer pulled her arm away. "What harm could come from listening to what he has to say?"

"None. Especially since he's probably going to tell you to be in the lab early to wash some test tubes or something." Jenna's words tumbled out in a hiss.

"Be quiet. You're just too harsh sometimes."

"I'm not harsh, Rumer. I'm real." Jenna glowered, but stopped talking. Dante was out of breath and was close enough for them to see an actual few beads of sweat on his brow. Rumer raised her eyebrows. He'd done a little work to catch up to them.

She folded her arms across her chest and waited, while Jenna stood back, an obvious scowl painted across her face.

"Ladies, how do you walk so fast in those shoes? I practically had to run to get to you." He stared straight at Rumer, and as soon as he unleashed his dimple, she softened. He locked his eyes on her. "Why'd you leave so fast?"

Rumer felt like a ten-year-old with a crush. She shrugged. Her face felt hot. She almost couldn't remember why they hadn't stayed longer.

Dante mimicked her shrug. "What is that? I thought I'd get to spend a few minutes with you, at the very least."

Her face felt hot. "You seemed busy."

Jenna crossed her arms in front of her chest "Let's go, girl. We have some work to do."

"I wasn't too busy for you." For the first time, Dante seemed to notice that Rumer wasn't alone. "How about this—" He rubbed his hands up and down Rumer's arms. "How about we take your friend home, and then you and I go to Thirteen Coins and get something to eat? My treat."

"It's the middle of the night. We have work to do," Jenna protested.

Dante locked eyes with Rumer, acting as if Jenna hadn't just spoken and his words were meant only for her. "The instructor has your back."

Rumer's voice was caught in her throat. How'd they get from annoyed at a party to this? She'd pictured them together, just not so soon. In her head, they'd talked on campus, take a few walks, grab a piece of pizza before. Then, maybe after at least a week, they'd go on a real date. In her head, she was in control of things, not caught up in some crazy whirlwind. It felt good. She blushed, then nodded.

A wide smile spread across Dante's face. "You're in good hands."

Rumer chuckled. "Like Allstate?"

"Better."

Rumer spied Jenna rolling her eyes. "What?" she asked?

"Nothing," her voice was barely above a mumble. "You seem too smart for this."

"Too smart for what?"

Jenna sighed heavily. "Never mind. Nothing."

Rumer narrowed her eyes, giving her friend a look. She would let her break that down more later. Jenna was being a hater. Right now, Dante was all she could concentrate on.

CHAPTER EIGHT

Rumer tried to read as she ate breakfast, but she couldn't concentrate. The Student Union had its normal hum going on, just above quiet, but not quite rowdy. The cast of characters did not deviate much day to day. Normally, she would spend some time people watching while she reviewed her work or read the news on her smart phone, but today nothing caught her attention for too long. Her thoughts were constantly interrupted by memories of Dante and the wonderful time they'd had last night.

From the moment they'd dropped Jenna at the dorms, Dante had been extra attentive, the exact opposite of how he'd acted at the party. He'd been the perfect gentleman. Chills ran through Rumer's body as she thought about it. He'd let her hold his arm while they walked. His forearm had been muscular, and it had taken everything Rumer had not to squeeze it as she rested her fingers there. They'd taken an Uber to Thirteen Coins, an all-night restaurant in downtown Bellevue. Rumer had only been there once before for brunch with her family and she'd never taken an Uber, especially not to the east side, although a lot of kids in her school had their own Uber accounts.

The lighting was low and the room they sat in was lit by small candles. The place was pretty busy, but since Dante seemed to know the hostess, he was able to score a table in the back in a corner, pretty much away from everyone else. She'd enjoyed the few hours they'd spent in semi-darkness. Instead of sitting across from her, Dante had slid into the booth next to her. It was slightly chilly in the place but he'd given off a heat that kept her warm for the entire two hours they'd been there.

Rumer replayed their conversation over and over in her mind. It was a little awkward at first and they'd started out talking about the class and robotics but their discussion had galloped all over the place: politics, school, movies, everything you could possibly think of. The conversation quickly became relaxed and natural, as if Dante was someone she'd known her entire life. He'd made her feel special and didn't seem at all intimidated by her being smart. That was the best part. Dante made her feel as if she could just talk about anything without explaining herself. She didn't have to pretend to be anyone other than who she was.

He'd paid the bill without even thinking about it, too. So fast, in fact, that Rumer barely had time to even offer to split it. She'd been very conscientious when she was ordering. She was on a limited budget, and it normally wouldn't include a place like Thirteen Coins. Whatever confusion she'd been feeling disappeared by the end of the evening. Now, there was no doubt in her head that Dante was feeling her, too.

Rumer was so lost in her thoughts, she didn't even notice when Jenna stomped over, not speaking. She plunked herself down beside Rumer so hard the table shook. Rumer barely looked up from the page she'd been staring at while she daydreamed, even when her Jenna let out a heavy sigh.

Jenna finally stopped her silent pouting. "Did you have a good time with our *instructor?*"

Rumer was jarred from her daydream. "You mean, Dante? Of course I did. I told you he was feeling me." She a sly smile spread across her face.

"Oh, I see. He's *Dante* now?" Jenna took a large inhale as if she needed a lot of air for what she was about to say. "He might be feeling you, but you really should play harder to get. I can't believe you ditched me for some dude that barely spoke to you after he invited you to a party. Did you even notice that he brushed you off in front of his friends? Do you remember how hurt you were?" Jenna's face burned with anger. " I don't understand how you could let yourself be treated that way.

Rumer sat back in her chair, away from Jenna. Her verbal attack was almost overwhelming. She sighed. It had occurred to her that Jenna might be pissed off, but she'd quickly dismissed that thought last night. "Let's not, Jenna. I didn't ditch you. We took you home."

"Really? Let's review." Jenna folded her arms across her chest. "We went to a party together. On the way home, some guy you barely know wants to hang out, and you just leave me and go, without us even discussing it. I call that being ditched. You deposited me at the dorms, like I was a pet you were dumping at a kennel or something. If he was any good, he would have taken us both out. He shouldn't have had any problem being around your friends. I'm not trusting him." Jenna pulled a book from her backpack, a scowl still on her face.

Rumer looked down at her plate and pushed her eggs around with her plastic fork. "Are you done?" Maybe she had ditched her friend, but she should understand, right? "I would've been okay with going back to the dorm if things had been the other way around. I wouldn't want to be a third wheel." Rumer heard her words, but she wasn't sure she believed them herself.

"You aren't me." Jenna glared. They had known each other a very long time, and other than the kid in fourth grade that wanted them both as a girlfriend at the same time, they'd never had this type of beef before. Even then, their fight hadn't really been about the guy. "I thought we were better than fighting over a dude, because it feels like that it what we are doing."

Rumer's face felt hot. "Look, I'm sorry. I didn't think that you would be upset."

Jenna didn't appear to be ready to give up so easily. She leaned in. "You're right, you didn't think." She paused and turned the page on her book so hard she almost ripped it. "I think it's nice that you found the new you and all, but not all that much was wrong with the old Rumer. She was smart and made good decisions—"

"Don't forget boring. And badly dressed."

"None of those things are true. You're thoughtful. And you dressed just like the rest of us, and I was fine with that. I don't know what made you decide you have to keep up with that picture in your head where everyone walks around looking like Beyoncé or Ciara. Even those people don't look that way without Photoshop."

Rumer fought back a feeling of sadness, but she had no idea why. Sure, Jenna had liked the way she was before, but she hadn't liked herself. "I think maybe, people just don't like change. With the old me, you knew what to expect. You knew how people would react to me, and you liked it. I was never the center of attention, always the sidekick. Maybe even your sidekick, and you liked me in that place. I'm tired of being that girl."

"What the hell? I'm going to stop you right there before you say anything more stupid. I don't know who dubbed you a psychologist, but you're still just like me, a dumb high school girl who doesn't know anything," Jenna fumed. "I don't want to fight with you about this. I don't understand why it isn't okay for you to just be you. Some of us will never be one of the popular kids, and we need to be fine with that. You and I, we're the smart ones. The ones that will have a life after all this school stuff is over."

Rumer waved her away. "Alright, *Alma*. Stop it."

Jenna's eyes got small. "I don't sound anything your mother."

"If you tell me that I'm not the type that men like, so I'd better study, I will hit you. I'm sorry about last night. Does that make you feel better? Can we talk about something else? Maybe the assignment we have to finish?"

"Fine. Won't bring it up again. You just be careful, that's all I'm going to say." Jenna's eyebrows were sky high by now. They gave away all of the things that her lips wouldn't say.

They didn't talk about it anymore, but Jenna was still making angry faces at her friend when they were interrupted.

"Hey, is this seat taken? You don't mind if me and my girls sit here, do you?" She didn't wait for an answer, instead, plopping down in the chair on either side of Jenna and Rumer.

Rumer stiffened. There were plenty of other empty chairs in the Student Union. Why in the world would anyone choose to be right up under them? She bit her lip, but still moved the papers she'd spread over the table out of the way and made room for the new additions. Both girls acted as if there were an imaginary wall between them and the other people at the table, but they couldn't help but notice the tons of hair and makeup. There must be twenty pounds of hair between them, Rumer thought. The beef between Rumer and her friend was just about forgotten. The addition of the other young women somehow united them.

"I'm Ranisha. You two are new, right? Freshman?" Ranisha's smile was saccharine sweet.

It took a minute for the girls to realize that they were the ones she was talking to. Ranisha chuckled at the surprise on both faces. "Um, yes. Sort of. We're taking a summer special science program."

"I see. *Smart* girls." Ranisha and her friends exchanged glances, their eyebrows raised. "That's really special. I didn't get your names." A nervous giggle escaped from her friend's lips.

They introduced themselves, and passed half-smiles around the table. The group created a dead spot in the room, and a silent bubble enveloped them. Rumer fidgeted, bouncing her pen off the table as she stared down at her notebook. She and Jenna exchanged glances, quickly looking away from each other before the girls, now sitting between them, noticed. Over-friendly people made Rumer uncomfortable. Neither one of them knew these people. She didn't feel as if they'd said everything they needed to, but they could continue their conversation later. She crossed her arms in front of her. They'd gone almost all summer without any people talking to them in the Student Union. Why now?

Ranisha played with the long silver necklace that hung down her front and sat back in her chair. "I thought I saw you at a party last night?"

Rumer's eye lit up. "Oh yeah, we were there. A friend invited us. We didn't stay long, though." She took a deep breath to keep herself from talking too fast. Now, she understood the sudden friendliness.

At the mention of the party, Jenna was back to glaring at her friend, her lips pursed.

"Really? You missed it then," Ranisha said. "That party turned up! We had a great time. My boyfriend and his friends know how to throw a party." She laughed and her friends nodded in concert with her. "I think we went way late, right, girl?" Both of her sidekicks nodded and smiled as if they had a secret that no one else was privy to.

Ranisha continued, not really expecting anyone else to join in on the conversation. "You know, I really didn't want to go, since Dante and I had been hanging out before the party, and all. We were just kicking it at his apartment a few minutes before—"

Rumer gasped.

"What? Is everything okay?" Ranisha asked. "Did I say something wrong?" She placed her fingertips on her chest and looked wide-eyed.

Rumer shook her head. "Nothing's wrong. Excuse me. Something was caught in my throat." *Could she possibly mean that Dante was her boyfriend?*

"Okay, well, as I was saying, we almost didn't go, but Dante had promised his friends that he would be there and he'd invited all of these people. Students. People like that. He likes to do that to make people feel comfortable here. What could I do? I just go along with him sometimes." Ranisha rambled on as if she didn't have a care in the world.

Her friend nodded. "I get that."

Jenna suddenly spoke up. "Oh. It's nice that you do stuff because of him. That must make him happy." She glared at Rumer, making a face. The conversation was getting juicier every minute they listened. Both she and Rumer were getting an earful they hadn't planned on.

"Ha." Ranisha leaned in. "You think this is about him?" she shook her head. "Girl, it's about *me*. I've got to protect what's mine." She high-fived her friend. "All the thirsty chicks out there? My man is fine as hell, and these chicken heads come around and think they can cheese all up in Dante's face, like he might want them or something. But let me tell you something, there is no *next*. We're going strong with no end in sight. They can come around him all they want, but they are going to be waiting a real long time. Dante is my boo." She paused. "I get it, though. It's real easy for people to develop a crush on him, especially those who don't know. He's not hard to look at or look up to, you know what I mean?"

"Wow." Jenna locked eyes with Rumer. "Sounds like a lot of work."

"Wow is right. He's worth it."

Rumer's face was hot with embarrassment. She gathered her things and began to stuff them back into her bag. "I just remembered. I have to go. I need to swing by the library before class. You coming, Jenna?"

"S-s-sure." Jenna hopped up. "I think I could benefit from visiting the library, too."

A broad smile spread across Ranisha's face. "Really? But we were just getting to know each other." She smirked.

"I know, right?" Rumer said. "It was a pleasure to meet you both." She turned to leave, her back tense.

"The pleasure was all mine." Ranisha sat back in her chair and watched until both girls disappeared through the doors of the Student Union. As soon as the doors swung shut, her smile disappeared from her face as if turned off by a switch.

"You think they got the picture?" One of the sidekicks asked.

"They're smart girls. I couldn't have made things any clearer. That girl is going to stay so far away from Dante now, he's going to think he has a bad case of body odor. I doubt she'll be a problem anymore."

"I know that's right."

Ranisha nodded. "I do know. Otherwise, she will get what's coming to her, and I can assure you, it's nothing pretty. Not everybody is cut out for this."

CHAPTER NINE

In the summer, the locker room stayed almost as busy as it was during the regular school year. It was the first stop for many of the guys that stayed around for the summer semester. Dante headed that way as he usually did to begin his day. He could drop his stuff off, then planned to get a run in after he finished his first class.

The locker room door clanged open in response to Dante's push. The loud bang as it hit the wall temporarily stopped all conversations. People paused for a second, a few glaring at Dante.

He shrugged. "Sorry." His response was barely above a mutter.

People looked away quickly, then resumed what they'd been doing before, some giving Dante a look of annoyance at his loud intrusion.

Oblivious to the glares, Dante ignored the people around the entryway and made his way to his usual spot, at the back of the locker room. He and his friends preferred the corner area. It was more secluded than the front and harder for everyone to hear what they were saying. It wasn't like they had any state secrets, but Dante, like the others, appreciated the feeling of a little privacy.

Two of his friends were there already. Justin straddled the bench, his elbows leaning on his knees, while the other, Paul, rearranged things in his locker. They looked up when Dante entered, long enough to speak. "What's up?" they spoke in unison, like twins that could read each other's minds.

"Hey, hey!" They greeted each other with their signature handshakes. "Same stuff as yesterday. What's up with you?"

Paul shrugged. "Nothing much. You're the one that's the man. In fact, we aren't sure you should be in here. Don't you think you need to be using the faculty locker room?"

"Yeah, the special room with the carpeting, for the *important* folk?" Justin added.

"Why're you tripping?" Dante laughed. "They don't play jams like this is *that* locker room." He bopped his head to Lil Wayne, mouthing the words. "No incentive for me to go there."

"You just might be too smart to be hanging out in here."

"Yeah," Paul added. "Not to mention just too much of a baller. You have all of the ladies just wrapped around your finger, man. We can't be hanging with you. We might make you look bad." They seemed to be enjoying their taunting.

Dante paused. "So you all got jokes, right?"

"I don't know if I'm joking or not. You ran out of the party and left us. We didn't see you again. Where'd you go? Not to mention that you didn't even bother to answer my text messages."

"I'm sorry about that, man. My phone is acting funny. I'm not getting some messages until hours later."

"Riiight," they both said together.

"You think we buy that? You can keep that line for one of your women." Justin raised an eyebrow. "It's okay for you to have been busy with a lady."

Paul laughed. "Yeah, man. We know it's hard being a pimp." He slapped Dante on the back.

"Don't hate." Dante tried hard to suppress a smile. "I was busy."

"I bet you were. Grading papers, right?" They laughed. "We know how it can be."

"Y'all are wrong about that." Dante sighed. "I was enjoying myself with intelligent conversation."

"Bedroom conversation, I bet." They laughed again. "Again, who are you telling that mess to? We know you, man."

"You see? That's why I don't tell you knuckleheads anything. I was at a restaurant, having dinner and conversation with a young lady." Dante turned his back on them to open his locker.

"Really? We saw you blow Ranisha off and act like you were done with her. Are we supposed to believe that not that long after you were enjoying yourself with her intelligent conversation? She must be a glutton for punishment, or your game is a lot better than we thought."

Dante took their teasing in stride. He was used to the way his friends ribbed each other. "What do you mean? I never said I was with Ranisha." He couldn't resist a little pushback of his own. They would have to drag any further details out of him.

A moment of silence passed as the two men glanced at each other. Dante tried not to look too smug. It had been a while since he'd successfully shut them down.

"What, you don't believe me?" Dante straddled the bench. He was on a roll. "I left the party and caught up to that hottie, Rumer. I laid a little of this charm on her and then we took her friend back to the dorms. The two of us went out to eat. We stayed a long time, and then I took her back to the dorms, too. She's actually quite intelligent."

"Intelligent?" Paul and Justin said together.

"You have to stop doing that, or I'm going to start to think that there is only one brain between you. Y'all ain't even related, so stop saying the same stuff." He paused. "Why are you tripping, anyway?"

"No one is tripping. You left, then we saw Ranisha run out behind you. We thought that the two of you had reconciled or some shit."

Dante laughed. "I'm not thinking about that chicken head. I told you that. She is just something to do."

"You mean *someone* to do."

"Very funny. No, seriously, I didn't even see her. She may have left, but she didn't go with me."

"Okay," Paul said. "That may be. But since when do you talk about a woman being intelligent? You're the one that's all about a woman's assets. You haven't said one thing about—"

"About her body? Oh, Miss thing got body. She's got *all* that. I was trying to be a better person."

"Really? You been drinking?" Laughter erupted from Dante's friends.

He paused, waiting for them to calm down. "I see. More jokes.

It's all good."

"Yes, it is. And normally you tell us all about how good it is. So, what you're saying is, you have no desire to hit that?"

"I never said that. I never said that at all. You're both trippin'. It's just that I have a way I do things."

"Do tell, Professor. What way is that?"

"I plan to go slow. I have to draw her in, make her beg. She wants me, there is no doubt about that, but women like to feel like they are being wooed, and all that. Don't you read GQ?"

"And you're so sure that she will beg, huh? Now that is the confident Dante I know."

"Oh, she *will* beg. All the wooing convinces them that you know how to be a man. Keeps them in their place. I intend to do both, that's all I'm saying."

"Is that so? Woo her and then you'll be a man?"

"Oh yeah. Then, I'll be *the* man."

"Really? You sound like you live in the dark ages," Tyrone added.

Dante paused. He threw his bag into his now open locker and waited. He made them wait before he answered.

"Say what you want, but I don't see the ladies chasing behind you like they do me. You see how they get all twisted. When she admits to me that she wants all this, then, and only then, will I tap that!"

CHAPTER TEN

Rumer sprinted from the Student Union, just short of a run. She moved so fast, Jenna struggled to keep up, her cries of "wait, wait," practically trailed behind her, lost between her pants of breath. They were halfway across campus before Jenna was able to come within four strides of her friend.

Jenna grabbed Rumer's arm, stumbling on the cobblestones that lined the path across campus. "What is your problem? You aren't going to let that heifer scare you away, are you?"

The words stopped Rumer in her tracks. "What are you talking about? A minute ago, you were telling me how I was losing myself and saying that Dante was bad. Make up your mind." She wiped away the tear that perched on her cheek.

"I never said he was bad. I was trying to make the point that maybe he was bad *for* you, or maybe you want to be with him for the wrong reasons. But that was before."

Rumor's heartrate was starting to slow. After talking to Ranisha, she'd left the Union feeling a jumble of emotions, all at the same time. The conversation with Ranisha had taken all the good stuff she was feeling and turned it into something hurtful and frightening and threatening, tossed in with a little bit, not a lot, of anger. Now, the clouds in her head were starting to clear. "And you think differently now? He's suddenly better for me? You heard them. Ranisha is his girlfriend. A girlfriend that is more permanent than not. I don't want to be in the middle of that."

"Oh, no? Why, you don't want to get in the way of their happiness? Is that it?" Jenna's lips pursed as her mouth drew into a line. "If he was so happy, he wouldn't have been all up in your face." Her raised eyebrows challenged Rumer.

Rumer let out a heavy sigh. "You know, let no man put asunder?"

"That's *marriage*. From what I could tell, they ain't there yet. This is still love and war. And we know that all's fair in love and war, right?"

Perhaps, Rumer thought. She really didn't know what to think. Dante seemed like he was interested, but then to hear all this from a girl he obviously cared about. Ranisha, or whatever her name was, had known more about him than she did, so it must be true. The fact of the matter was that Rumer had only known Dante a few days.

"What's that? My friend Rumer is a fighter. I can't believe you would just give up so easily. Don't you think that Dante can make his own choice? If he wanted her, she would have been out with him, laughing and joking and dumping her best friend back at the dorms, instead of you."

Rumer forced back a smile. She wanted to believe that Jenna was right. If Dante wasn't interested, he wouldn't have stepped to her in the first place. But she really didn't want to make any enemies, and it sure felt as if Ranisha could be one she really didn't want to have.

She'd seemed so sure of herself. "You heard the way Ranisha was talking about Dante. They obviously have a *thing*." She wanted her college experience, no matter how short, to be different than high school. She was tired of being the girl on the outside and the butt of everyone's jokes, so that meant she didn't want to ruffle the wrong people's feathers. All it would take was one pissed off popular person, and she would be right where she'd been in high school; on the outside, looking in.

"Come on, girl. This isn't so different from what we're used to. That is what she wants you to believe, but I would withhold my judgment until I heard that from Dante himself." She paused. "Stop acting like you don't know the game, because you do. You're smarter than this. The real reason that girl came and sat with us was to intimidate you into crawling into a hole somewhere. She wouldn't have needed to do that if she and Dante were as tight as she tried to make us believe."

"I'm not so sure. She—"

"We know the type. She was threatened by you. And who wouldn't be? I know the same girl you were yesterday is hiding in there somewhere, but all she sees is a really pretty, intelligent person that has turned the head of her very attractive man. You can talk about robotics with him. She was trying to psych out her competition. Make you go away. Doesn't your mother tell us that the game isn't over until the fat lady sings?" She put her hand to her ear, as if to cup it. "I don't hear any singing."

"For real, Jenna? The fat lady? My mother is fifty million years old, too old for you to sound like her. This isn't some class I'm trying to get a good grade in."

"No, Rumer, it's not, but the same rules still apply. You have never let a no keep you from something you wanted before. Why are you going to start now? Just because she says that they're an item doesn't mean they are. She says she was at the party. If she is his girlfriend, why was he running behind you?"

Rumer shrugged again.

"One more shrug and I'll have to slap you back to yourself. *I hear no singing.* We're all grown-ups. This isn't high school any more. I say, let Dante chose what he wants to do. If last night is any indication, those two, if they ever really were an item, are just about over. That chick is desperate."

"Thirsty. You mean thirsty."

Jenna rolled her eyes. "Thirsty, desperate, whatever. My advice is the same. You can be the new star in his show if you want to be."

Jenna had a point, Rumer thought. It was *her* that had spent the night with Dante, not Ranisha. He'd chased *her* down the street. He'd invited *her* to the party. And he'd promised *her* that last night wouldn't be the last time they hung out. "Maybe you're right. Maybe all that stuff Ranisha was talking about was in her head only."

Jenna nodded. "You know we've met more than one delusional girl. That one could have all kinds of crazy fantasies in her head, but they would be just that, fantasies. People make up all sorts of crazy stuff all the time to make things seem closer to what they want to believe."

"Let's see what happens. It's not like I won't see him in class today. I'll just ask him when we talk later. I think he will just tell me what the deal is. What reason does he have to lie?"

No matter what their differences, Jenna had a way of making her feel better. Besides, when you stopped to think about it, what she was saying made a lot of sense. Jenna might be a pain sometimes, but she always had her back.

Rumer didn't get a whole lot of time to digest their conversation. Just as they rounded the corner that led to their classroom, Dante walked toward them. Rumer's heart skipped a beat. The pale blue polo shirt he was wearing let his muscular arms show from about a hallway away. A broad smile spread across her face, and her legs slowed down her walk by themselves. Rumer felt as if a fog had enveloped her, and the only thing she could see clearly was Dante. He was smiling.

"Hello ladies." His voice was hushed and professional and he spoke without looking directly at either of the girls. "I trust I'll see you in class today?" He stood apart from them, almost as if he was afraid to get too close.

Jenna's mouth fell open in surprise.

"You're mighty formal—" Rumer tried to contain the giggles that slipped from her lips.

"I hope you got to finish the assignment from the last class," Dante continued, not even acknowledging that Rumer had spoken at all.

A feeling of confusion spread throughout Rumer's head. Last

night, it had felt as if they had known each other forever. Now she felt like they should be addressing each other by last names only, almost as if she should be apologizing for even speaking to him.

She nodded slowly. "Of course," she stammered. She'd stayed up well after returning to the dorms to get her work done. She'd been way too excited to sleep anyway. Rumer crossed her arms in front of her. This was not how she'd expected to be greeted. She had imagined a slow, shy hello that left her blushing and maybe an awkward hug, or Dante's breath on her ear. She blinked. Nowhere in her daydreams had the picture looked like this. "Do you think I could talk to you for a bit?" Maybe he didn't want to talk in front of Jenna, but that even sounded crazy. Why would he suddenly be shy now?

Dante looked at his watch and cleared his throat. "I may have some time during office hours." He glanced at her, making eye contact for the first time. "*After* class."

Had she seen a wink? "After class? Like in your office?"

"I think that will be very busy. All of the TA's share one office. I can meet you in the robotics lab. About four? That way I can get everything you need answered. Will that work?"

Rumer nodded, unsure. Now they were back to mixed messages again. Did they have a thing? Or not? Or had she imagined the connection that she'd felt between them?

"Good," he said. Dante glanced at his watch again. "I'll see you ladies in class then."

They both stood, dumbfounded as he strode away. Jenna quickly recomposed herself. "Oh-kay. I really don't see what you see in him. He's a strange one. He might as well have added 'class dismissed' to the end of that. I mean, what was that?"

Rumer shrugged. "He's the professor now, remember? So maybe he has to act a certain way. I understand totally." She didn't even believe herself.

"And you're the only one. But I guess you're the only one that has to."

Rumer nodded, but her feelings were bruised. She'd been sure the next time they crossed paths, Dante would have walked up to her and planted one right on her cheek, or at least acted like he was glad to see her. Instead, she felt like some stranger that was asking him to spare a dollar at a busy intersection or something. If this was how things were going to be, she was going to have to do some adjusting to the fairy tale in her head.

CHAPTER ELEVEN

Dante barely made eye contact at all during his lecture, and almost completely ignored her when Rumer raised her hand to ask questions. Rumer's nose flared. He didn't choose her, instead he looked at her with his mouth drawn into a thin line, with not even a small hint of recognition. Defiant, she kept her hand in the air and Dante's eyes scolded her. Finally, her face hot, Rumer slowly let her hand shrink back down to the desk and folded them in front of her. She was so angry, she couldn't even take notes. By the time the class was over, she felt like she was a total nut and had completely imagined the vibe they'd had at the restaurant. Why was he doing this?

"Okay, see you all tomorrow. That's enough for today." Dante had barely dismissed them and she'd slid out the back door. She didn't wait for Jenna, instead waving goodbye when Jenna was busy talking to the girl that sat on her other side, so she wouldn't have an opportunity to stop her. She didn't even want to take the chance of walking passed Dante. He might have to act like the distant professor or whatever, but she wasn't sure she could take much more of what he was dishing out. He would clear things up later, she was sure of it.

As she made her way to the lab, she was barely able to concentrate. Rumer's mind was full of questions and remembrances of her impromptu date. Dante might have ignored her today, but she kept thinking about the warmth that had come off of his arm as he sat next to her in the restaurant, and the tingles that had run through her when his hand had touched hers. *That* had been real.

Rather than fight it, she decided to just go to the lab early. That way, she could get a jumpstart on her lab work and kill two birds with one stone. Maybe even pay attention to her work while he wasn't in the room. At the very least, she would try and force herself to concentrate on one thing for the time she had to wait.

The lab was almost empty, just as she'd been told it would be. There was only one other person there, and he didn't even appear to even notice her when she came in. Rumer chose a spot on the far side of the room. The only person she wanted to talk to was Dante, and it would be well over an hour before he would arrive.

The laboratory stool made a scraping sound on the concrete floor as Rumer pulled it out from under the table, echoing throughout the almost empty room. Rumer plunked her heavy robotics book onto the table, ignoring the dust that rose from it. She put her headphones in her ears, sighed and tried to block everything else out. Rumer immersed herself in the chapter. Before long, she was lost in her work. She almost jumped out of her skin when she felt someone tap her on the shoulder. As she jumped up, the stool she'd been sitting on clanged to the floor, and she had to grab the window sill to avoid falling over it.

The guy from the other corner of the lab was standing over her, his hands in the air as if someone were pointing a gun toward him. "I'm sorry. I didn't mean to startle you. I said excuse me a few times, but you seemed to be deep in it."

Her heart was beating so loudly that she almost couldn't hear his words. Rumer breathed heavily, her hand over hear heart. "You really shouldn't sneak up on people like that."

"And you shouldn't leave your headphones in and your music up so loud that you aren't aware of your surroundings." He raised his eyebrow. "These labs can be very deserted." His eyes locked onto hers in silent challenge. They didn't even know each other and it felt as if they were in the middle of some impasse, waiting to see who would be the quicker draw.

"Did you want something?"

He paused, running his hand over the top of his head. "I'm sorry. I didn't mean to startle you. Let me start over. I'm Paul. I saw you over here and wanted to say hello."

A look of confusion spread over Rumer's face. "Okay?"

"We met last night? At the party?"

Rumer nodded, but racked her brain for some recollection. He didn't look familiar to her at all.

Paul pointed to himself. "Dante's friend? He introduced us when you came in?"

She still didn't remember his face, but forgave his intrusion with her weak smile. "I'm sorry." She vaguely remembered that someone had been standing behind Dante at the party when she first saw him. "It was a long night."

"I get it. No worries. I wanted to holler at you—"

"A holler would have been better from across the room."

His mouth dropped open. "Wow. You bite."

Rumer's face softened a bit. She hadn't intended to be so harsh.

"I would have said something earlier, but like I said, you looked busy, and you left the party so early."

She nodded. "I did. Dante and I—"

He held up his hand to stop her. "You don't have to explain to me. Your business is your business. I was taking an opportunity when I saw it."

"An opportunity?"

"Yes, an opportunity to say a few words to a fine young lady."

Rumer laughed. What was his game? "I just told you—"

"Yeah, I know. That you and Dante hung out. But you never know. He's my boy, but he has so many *friends*, I thought I'd check anyway. Thought maybe you and I could hang out some."

What did he mean by that? So many friends? "Really?" Was he really trying this?

"Yeah, you never know with that one. But it's all good. My loss." He bowed. "You be careful, okay? I wouldn't want to see a sweet girl like you get hurt."

What the hell? "I'm sorry, but I don't recall asking for your opinion, advice or commentary." Was he implying that there was some danger she didn't know about? Why was her love life suddenly the subject of so much concern? "I can take care of myself—"

Rumer's retort was interrupted by the lab door opening. They both looked up to see Dante striding toward them. Unlike earlier, a broad smile rested on his face. "Rumer!" His voice resounded through the lab. "I'm sorry it took me so long." He looked over at Paul. "Hey, wassup, man. I didn't know you'd be here. You two know each other?" He looked from Rumer to Paul.

"Not really, I was just saying hello. I saw this fine lady over here by herself, studying hard. Looks like you're working them already. I didn't know you two were meeting here."

Dante ignored Paul's comment. "That's good, you got a head start. We do have to get down to business." He turned to Rumer and ran his tongue along his top lip.

"I know what you mean," Paul said. "I'd like to work on her myself."

Rumer blushed and looked away. *What the hell?*

Dante gave his friend a weird look, as if he hadn't heard correctly. "Nah, man. There won't be any of that." Any anger she'd felt from his earlier treatment had faded away as soon as he'd smiled at her.

Paul frowned. "Oh, I thought she was one of your *students.*" Sarcasm dripped from his voice.

Dante paused, his face darkening. "You know what, Paul, would you excuse us?" He cleared his throat. "We really do have a lot of work to get done. Rumer is going to be working on my project and we don't need any distractions."

"Okay, I get it. No distractions. It's time for me to go, anyway. Nice meeting you again, Rumer. My offer still stands." He winked.

"And you be safe, okay?" They were silent as he backed away, packed his stuff and left.

Rumer nodded and then looked away, not wanting to think about any possible hidden meaning in his comment about being safe. *And what offer?* She played with her pen. *He couldn't have meant that lame comment he'd made earlier?*

"So," Dante finally spoke, his one word filling up the space of a whole paragraph. He stepped closer to her. "I couldn't wait to get to see you again. And I'm sorry about earlier. I figured you might not want everyone all in your business."

"So that was it. I was confused." Relief washed over her. She knew that there had to be a logical explanation. "And my feelings were kind of hurt."

"I apologize. Since we will be working so closely together, I know it can be hard. Our relationship in the lab will be intimate, and other people might not understand."

Rumer nodded. It was clear that Jenna certainly did not.

"You're a brilliant woman. I think it's important for us to get to know each other better. I find that a connection on a more personal level will help the ideas flow."

"Really? Is that what you had with Ranisha? A more *personal* connection?" Rumer's eyes grew wide as soon as the words slipped from her mouth. That was a mistake. She didn't want to push him away before they even got started.

A look of surprise flickered on Dante's face, and then disappeared. He cocked his head to the side. "Ranisha and I are friends. She's not a robotics student, if that's what you mean."

Is that what he called it? Friends? That answer left Rumer wanting more details. It didn't seem like Ranisha understood that.

Dante leaned in. "I can help you get the most out of this project. It will make your college applications so much stronger."

She drew in her breath. The project? No more about Ranisha? Why wouldn't he just tell her what she wanted to know? She inhaled. He smelled too good to be true. Rumer readied herself for whatever came next. If he tried to kiss her, she was ready. She'd been ready. It felt like a kiss was coming. The air in the room stood still.

Instead of the kiss Rumer was anticipating, Dante strode around the lab worktable and pulled up a stool. It made a dull thumping sound as the rubber feet thudded across the floor. He pulled her book closer to him. "So, we should get started. We only have two weeks left to get this done. You can program a Raspberry Pi, right?" He referred to the small circuit board that would be the brain of their project, the smallest type of computer.

Rumer's heart sank. "Yes, of course." She fought back tears, but joined Dante at the table. This was not how this lab conversation was supposed to go. She'd imagined that they would talk about Ranisha, reminisce about last night, and then discuss the wonderful plans they would be doing later, but she supposed they would have to get some work done, too. "Can I ask you a question before we start?" Her throat was so parched that she was barely able to get the words out.

"Oh, sure. It's about the code, right? Well…" Dante turned the pages on the book and started talking so fast that Rumer didn't have time to even respond. Her question wasn't about coding or accessibility or robotics. She wanted to know about Ranisha, but it could wait. She didn't want to seem thirsty. That might drive him away, and now that she had a man like Dante interested, she didn't want that.

CHAPTER TWELVE

Rumer settled down and pushed her questions about Ranisha to the back of her mind. She and Dante worked until late, and before she knew it, it was close to eight and getting dark. They moved from book to lab table and they were so deep in the research project that neither noticed the night creep in.

The work really was fascinating. Rumer was in awe of Dante; he had the answers to every question she had and explained things to her in a way that made everything easy for her to understand. She watched him as he went through the information she needed for the project. He carefully pointed out diagrams and drew pictures on her notebook that helped her to grasp the information without any problems.

She nodded in response to most of his questions and tried hard to concentrate, but she couldn't keep her thoughts in check. The way he ran his tongue over his delicious-looking lips was distracting, but he didn't get angry when she asked him to slow down or explain again.

Her phone was on silent, but the flashing of her ring notification lit up the dark corner of the room where she'd left it. The only lights were from the lamps where they were working, and, at first, Rumer mistook the flash for lightning. She jumped, almost dropping the wires she held in her hand.

"Calm down. It's just your phone." Dante laughed at her without apology. "Aren't you a little high-strung? I would have never guessed that about you."

"I didn't expect the flash to be so bright." Rumer picked up the phone and looked at the screen. "It's almost nine PM. That was Jenna. She's probably wondering where I am. I never stay gone this long." She laughed nervously. "We kind of keep track of each other." She pressed redial to call her friend.

"I guess we should be finishing up anyway. This is no way to spend a Friday night."

She almost hated to admit it, but she'd be just fine if they spent the rest of the evening holed up in the lab, just like this. Rumer put the phone to her ear, and Jenna answered on the first ring. Rumer started talking immediately to try and head off the complaints she knew were coming. She'd be annoyed, too, if Jenna disappeared and she hadn't from her in hours. "I'm coming soon. I'm in the lab." She kept her voice just above a whisper.

"Still? I thought we were going to get dinner? You left class without telling me anything, so I really had no idea what you planned to do. What's up with that? It felt like you were sneaking away again. Thank you for keeping me in the loop." Sarcasm dripped from Jenna's voice.

"I'm sorry for that." Rumer watched as Dante started to shut things down. "We're cleaning up now. If you still want to, we can go eat."

Dante's ears perked up. "Ask her if she wants to go to the movies."

"Tell your boyfriend that I have no desire to be the third wheel," Jenna answered back as if she were in the room.

"You wouldn't be the third wheel. And don't you know that common protocol calls for you to wait for me to relay what the other person is saying before you answer." She frowned. They hadn't discussed any movies. Or was he trying to take Jenna on a date now? And had he heard Jenna refer to him as her boyfriend? Rumer's face reddened.

"Protocol? That went out the window a long time ago, like when you ditched me last night. Why would I do that? It sounds like he's right up under you, so I know he can hear everything I say."

Rumer sighed. Jenna had to go *there*. She'd never been one to let things go easily.

"She won't be the third wheel," Dante practically yelled from across the room where he was busy putting things away. "We'll invite my boy, too. We can double date."

Rumer's voice caught in her throat. *Double what?* She'd just taken three hours to get over confusion of who was what to whom, and now Dante was changing it up again. He was acting like they were all couply and everything, rather than two people who'd worked on a project together for hours with only one of them daydreaming about a romance. Either he wasn't attracted to her, or he was really good at controlling his emotions, much better than she was.

Jenna started chattering away, but Rumer muted the phone. "I'm sorry, I don't recall anything about a *single* date."

"You are so right. My apologies. I thought that we worked so hard that maybe you might want to catch a movie or something."

"It's the 'Or something' that I am worried about."

He laughed. "Was I being presumptuous?" He raised one eyebrow. "I promise, I'm harmless."

Rumer didn't answer, but her lips curled into a smile. She put the phone by her ear. "Jenna? Sorry. Anyway, movies, maybe?" She couldn't believe herself. Yes, she was confused, but she really liked the idea of going somewhere, anywhere with Dante, and it didn't matter whether they were alone or with other people. All her emotions were jumbled up together again. It felt like a repeat of last night.

"What friend?" Jenna asked. "'Cause you know I don't do charity cases. There's always something wrong with them if they need to be fixed up."

She turned away from Dante and cupped her hand over her mouth so that he couldn't hear what she was about to say to her friend. "That could go both ways, Missy."

"Look," Jenna said. "I don't need to be fixed up. I'm doing this as a favor, and I don't have patience right now to be saddled with some pitiful person."

"You're not marrying him, you're just going to the movies."

"Tell her he's nice looking, tall and smart." Dante was smiling broadly. "Isn't that what you ladies are about nowadays? If we pick you up in an hour, we can make the last show."

Dante knocked on Rumer's dorm room at exactly 9:22. The thump reverberated throughout the small room and Jenna jumped, almost poking herself in the eye with her mascara wand. "Why aren't they meeting us downstairs?" she asked, whispering almost too loudly. "We can't let a bunch of strangers into our dorm room, especially male strangers. And certainly not when it looks a mess like this." She waved her arm around.

Rumer shrugged, putting the finishing touches on her lips. "He insisted. Said something about it being safer if he came up." She blinked at herself in the mirror and double-checked her handiwork, taking a deep breath. "Do I look okay?"

"That's as good as it's going to get," Jenna said. "Are you going to answer the door? You're the puppet master in all of this, so you should be the one to let your man in."

"He's not my man."

"Not yet. Get the door!"

"Not before my face is on point. I don't want him to be able to take his eyes off of me." She pouted at the mirror some more, practicing her selfie-lips.

Jenna frowned. "Girl, whatever. We're just going to the movies. Isn't that what you told me earlier?" She stood behind Rumer, staring at her in the mirror from over her shoulder. "Enough already. You don't want him wasting his money by spending all of the time looking at you instead of what we're going to see. Did we decide what that was?"

Rumer shrugged. "Doesn't really matter, does it?"

Dante knocked again.

"I'll get it. You fix yourself. He's kind of impatient. All I know is that his friend better be good looking, or you owe me big."

Jenna opened the door and Dante's smile took both her and Rumer's breath away. Rumer couldn't help but stare. If she'd thought that he looked good before, Dante looked good enough to eat now, and he smelled good, too. Rumer drew in her breath. She could barely eke out a hello.

Dante poured on the charm, smiling just enough to reveal his dimple. The hallway lighting glinted off his freshly shaven and moisturized skin. "Are you ladies ready?" He didn't flinch, acting as if people reacted the way Rumer did to him on a daily basis.

Rumer nodded slowly, noticing that Dante let his eyes roam slowly over her, from head to toe. How was it possible for him to practically take her breath away and they'd just met? Dante exuded confidence and he was attractive. There was no way she could not be totally smitten. "You approve?"

"I do," Dante answered. "Almost perfect."

"What? Almost?"

"I wouldn't want your head to get too big. Give you some room to grow." Dante flashed a grin, enjoying his own cleverness.

"Where's your friend?" Jenna looked around Dante to see if someone else was standing in the hallway, but it was empty.

"Paul is downstairs. He didn't think he should come up since he hadn't met you, and he mentioned that he and Rumer hadn't gotten off to the best of beginnings." He raised his eyebrows, looking for a reaction from Rumer.

Jenna glared at her friend. "I thought you hadn't met this person?"

"I didn't realize I had, but at least he seems thoughtful." Rumer's brow furrowed. She didn't exactly have good feelings when she'd met Paul. First, he snuck up on her. Then, when he knew she had been in the lab to meet Dante, she still felt like he was hitting on her. What kind of person did that to his friend? The hairs on the back of her neck bristled.

Jenna noticed the look on her friend's face. "All good?"

"Yes." Rumer nodded too fast. She didn't say anything else, but it was just the movies, right?

Dante escorted them down to the lobby, and all the while, Jenna's nervousness was almost palpable. She stood way too close to Rumer in the elevator, shaking her leg in a way that vibrated them both. Rumer reached down and pressed the tips of her index finger into Jenna's leg to stop her, squeezing her friend's hand in support. How bad could this be? Paul was no Dante, but he hadn't been hard on the eyes that she remembered.

Paul was waiting outside the residence hall front door. Dante made introductions, and Jenna visibly relaxed. Her eyes flickered over his body, taking in his square jawline and his neat shoulder-length locks. They framed his cocoa-brown face and impossibly long eyelashes. After she'd taken in the whole picture, she let out the breath she had been holding for the past five minutes. This might not be too bad. She'd only been on a few dates, but on television, blind dates were mostly terrible. So far, so good. At least he wasn't bad to look at. All she could do was hope that her good fortune would continue.

"So this is my lovely date for the evening?" Like Dante, his dimple showed when he smiled, revealing his perfectly straight teeth. Paul took Jenna's hand when she extended it, kissing it without taking his eyes off of her face. She blushed and giggled, enjoying every bit of attention.

Rumer glared at her friend. What happened to the hard girl who didn't want to date a charity case? Where was the skeptic who thought everyone was out to game everyone else first? And the one that had been so nervous in the elevator she'd practically shaken the entire elevator car with her nervous leg? Rumer rolled her eyes. One glance at a pretty face and Jenna was putty, just about to throw her panties in Paul's face. There was so much more to a person than the way he looked.

No matter what her first impression had been, Rumer had to admit that Paul was very attractive. He dripped tall, dark and handsome, and his features were so symmetrical, they were unsettling. His eyes had a sparkle to them that made you think that he was generally a happy person inside and he smelled good, just like Dante did. She hadn't noticed that earlier, but that didn't mean a thing. He could still have the personality that could override all of that fineness. No matter how good-looking someone was, a bad attitude could make them seem like the most unattractive person in the room.

"And you two have met," Dante left his sentence open at the end, raising his eyebrows. He locked eyes with Paul, as if he was warning him to be on his best behavior. There was an awkward pause for a second, and then Paul extended his arms toward Rumer.

"Yes, we're old friends, and old friends get hugs." He enveloped Rumer into an embrace, whispering in her ear. "I thought I'd help keep you out of trouble."

Rumer squirmed free. "I'm good. I told you before, I can take care of myself." A chill ran through her. What was his deal? He'd held onto her for just a second too long, long enough to make her radar go up. A hugger? She'd have to keep an eye on this one, for sure.

The Sundance Theater was a short walk from the campus. Neither Rumer nor Jenna had been there before, but they'd both wanted to go. In addition to movies, they served real food and had a bar, and going made the movies more of a special occasion.

They looked at each other as they walked up. Normally, you had to be eighteen to get in, or at least with an eighteen-year-old, and both of them were nowhere near that. They'd watched their older friends go for years, and although it was close, a fancy movie theater that had higher-than-normal ticket prices and served real food like an actual restaurant wasn't really in their student budgets. A moment of silence passed between the two friends and anticipation hung heavy in the air.

They lagged behind their dates as they approached the box office. Dante hadn't really said they were coming to the expensive movie place and Rumer wasn't sure he planned to pay. She kicked herself, wishing she'd thought about discussing this before. She grimaced at Jenna, and her friend automatically knew that she was adding up the money in her checking account in her head. If she had to pay for both of them, she would have to call home and ask her mother for more money to last the rest of the summer, or she'd be relegated to only eating Top Ramen in the dorms. As much as they loved Starbucks, that just didn't seem like a great option. Things were tight at home as it was. She'd rather starve than ask her mother for more money because she'd spent what she had on a trip to the movies. Rumer could hear her mother as clearly as if she were standing right beside her. "I didn't send you up there to be hanging out and going to the fancy movies. I haven't even been to the fancy movies. You're supposed to be studying, not hanging out."

Dante turned around and smiled, drawing Rumer out of her thoughts. He reached his hand back in their direction. "Why are you walking way back there? I got you."

Rumer and Jenna exchanged a furtive glance as Rumer melted, relieved. Dante got better by the minute. Her fantasy was a tall, smart, good-looking man who was a gentleman, and gentlemen never let women pay. She took his hand, taking a few quick steps to catch up to him. She let her hand slide into his warm one. Rumer smiled and held on tight.

"We didn't talk about this, but you ladies will let this be our treat, right?" Dante said.

Paul led Jenna forward by her elbow. "Yeah, I remember how it was when I was your age. Every dime counts."

Dante glared at his friend. He leaned back and whispered to Paul. "Let the age thing, go, Man. They are both so fine, age really doesn't number."

"Yeah, whatever," Paul lowered his voice, too, but kept a smile on his face.

"I thought we had an agreement."

Rumer tried to keep a straight face, but couldn't help but overhear. "Don't tell me you're going to treat us like babies, now? We're almost legal."

Jenna scowled. "Almost," she said.

"Don't give me that look," Paul said. "Being a starving student is hard. Hell, I'm about to graduate, I have a job, and it's still hard for me."

Dante softened. "Yes, it's hard out here for a pimp, right?" He pushed his credit card through the ticket window and they all laughed easily.

"Where have I heard that before?" Paul's eyes were locked on Dante's and Rumer looked from one to the other as they laughed together. She felt as if there was something she was missing, but didn't want to seem young, so she let it go. The tension between them did seem to ease, and the nagging feeling in the back of her mind faded. Dante's joke had relaxed both sides, even if it was only a little.

The theater was dimly lit, but even without a lot of light, Rumer could tell that it was very clean. She held onto Dante's hand, standing slightly behind him as he handed the tickets to the woman in the stool by the door. Rumer tried not to stare, but the woman had tattoos covering every inch of visible skin. There was even a snake that wrapped from her ear and down across her throat. A phone earpiece blinked just over her ear. Rumer tore her eyes away, forcing herself to look at Jenna instead.

The sound of Rumer's sandals slapping the concrete floor was loud in her ears and her heart beat hard, magnified in her head. She couldn't shake the feeling that she somehow didn't belong. Part of her was worried that the woman would challenge them or ask for identification. She needn't have worried, though. The ticket taker barely looked at either one of them, instead taking their tickets and absentmindedly ripping them in half.

Dante guided them past the bar. There were six people seated there, but no one turned around as the group slinked past and back to their theater. As they passed, Rumer spotted the top of the bartender's head, noting that she was a female. They paused inside the door for their eyes to adjust.

Cartoons played as part of the pre-pre show. Rumer smiled as they slid into the bigger-than-normal movie chairs. The cartoon man on the screen dropped an engagement ring off the end of the pier as she settled into the chair. Dante sat next to her, immediately raising the adjustable arm so they could sit closer. He smiled. "I don't want anything between us." Rumer's face burned. Instead of another row of seats, there was a bench-like table in front of them.

"I hope you're hungry," Dante said as he picked up the thin menu. He turned to Paul, who was sitting on the other end of their group, on the other side of Jenna. "You want a beer, man? I got it."

Paul shook his head. "No."

"Why? It's not like we're driving home. You can have one."

Paul looked at Jenna. "I could, but I was trying to be respectful of the young ladies." He raised his eyebrows as if using them to point in Rumer's direction.

Dante was silent for a second, then he finally caught on. "Oh, right. Unless they don't mind. I'm sure it won't be the first time they had a drink."

"You are so thick sometimes. No, I'm sure it won't be. But the waitress comes right here and looks in your face. I'm sure it won't be the first or the last time they get carded, either."

Rumer spoke up. "You can drink if you want to. It won't bother me one way or the other. You do you, right Jenna?"

Even in the dim light, Jenna's embarrassment was obvious. She nodded, too quickly. "That's right. I'm good with iced tea."

Dante sneered at his friend. "Well, iced tea it is then. For all of us." He scribbled angrily on the ordering pad in front of them, not looking at Paul again.

"What's your issue?" Paul asked.

Dante sighed. "No issue. You just need to be cool." His voice was low. "You're killing the mood, acting like you're somebody's daddy." He glared at his friend. Paul looked away, instead concentrating on the screen.

Rumer enjoyed the warmth of Dante's arm around her shoulders for the entire movie. He pulled her close, so much so that she had a hard time concentrating on anything but him. She daydreamed, imagining his kiss and replaying the things he'd said on their first date. She reimagined the feeling she'd had when he'd held her hand earlier outside the movie theater, over and over. Before she knew it, the movie was over and she had no idea what it was actually about. When the lights came up, she felt as if the time had passed so quickly that it took a moment for her to hide her surprise.

Jenna looked at her strangely as Dante stood up and stretched. "What did you think?" he asked, looking at Rumer as if she were the only one he cared to hear reply.

"It was good," she answered, hoping that he couldn't tell she had no idea if the movie was good or not. She'd missed most of it, frolicking in her day dreams instead of paying attention to the screen.

Paul grabbed the bill and Dante reached for his wallet at the same time. "We can split this," he said. "I'm surprised they haven't come for this already. They usually do before the end credits." A waiter had brought their drinks and food, but he was nowhere in sight.

As if on cue, a different waitress ran up with a payment machine in hand. She fiddled with it without looking up. "Sorry, we're short— " She stopped midsentence.

Both Dante and Paul were paused with their credit cards in midair. Rumer's eyes had been fixed on Dante and she was puzzled for a split second. Dante stared at the waitress as if frozen.

"Wow. I can't believe you." She spat her words like a bad taste in her mouth.

A jolt of recognition struck Rumer. Ranisha was standing in front of them, obviously pissed off. She'd folded her arms across her chest, now heaving, and her eyes were locked on Dante.

Dante seemed to fumble for a second, then spoke. "Hey, Ranisha. I didn't expect for you to be here." He tried to be all sweetness and smiles.

His sweetness was lost on Ranisha. "Apparently not. I switched shifts with someone else." She switched her gaze to Rumer. " I see why you didn't call me."

"Let's not, Ranisha." He held up his hand in a stop sign motion, a sharpness replacing the saccharine in her voice that had been there just a few seconds before.

By now, Jenna had moved around the men and stood next to her friend. "You know, it looks like you have some things to work out. We're gonna go." She grabbed Rumer's hand, pulling her away.

Ranisha and Dante ignored them both. "Let's not. That's not what you told me—"

She didn't get to finish her sentence. In a split second, Dante reached out and grabbed Ranisha's wrist, practically snatching her over the table and into their row. "You seem to be forgetting who you are talking to, woman. I will call you when I'm ready." He emphasized every word of his last sentence in an effort to drive his meaning home.

Ranisha struggled to stay on her feet. Dante had practically snatched her so that her toes were just barely touching the floor. She used her other hand to brace herself on the table, attempting to pull herself in the opposite direction.

Rumer gasped. Dante's face had darkened and changed so much that he looked like an entirely different person. Jenna covered her mouth with her hand.

"Dante." Paul's voice was low and calm. "Not a good look, man." He looked around to see who was paying attention.

His friend's voice pulled Dante out of the dark space he'd gone to. "Don't ever step to me like that again." He spoke with a clenched jaw, forcing the words out between his teeth. This time, he let Ranisha wrench herself free.

She glared at him, then cut her eyes at Rumer and shook her head. "You just don't know." She took a breath and smoothed the black apron she was wearing, then turned her attention to the credit card machine that she'd stuffed in her apron pocket. Ranisha pressed a button, but nothing happened. Frustrated, she shook the machine, all the while looking as if she were fighting back the tears that were trying to escape from her eyes. "You got cash? My credit card machine is busted." Her voice cracked.

Dante's eyes never moved from Ranisha's face. "I'll meet you ladies outside." He clenched his fists, opening and closing them repeatedly.

Paul looked from Dante to Ranisha. "We're done here, right? I got this one." He ruffled through his wallet, hurriedly counting out bills as he spoke.

"Nah, I think I need to talk to this young lady. Remind her of some things. It won't take me that long. Rumer, I'll be out in just a few." Dante dismissed Rumer and turned back to Ranisha.

As Jenna led her friend out of the theater, they were both at a loss for words. She didn't like the tone in Dante's voice and didn't want to wait to be asked to leave again. She wanted to get away from Dante and his drama as fast as she could, and Rumer was coming with her whether she wanted to or not. She didn't let her friend go until they'd reached the front of the building.

"Can you believe that? He seems to have all kinds of drama following him," Jenna said. "I mean, who does that?"

Rumer paced in front of the theater, staring down at her feet. She stopped. "Who does what? You mean interrupting our date? I agree then because Ranisha knew that we were on a date. She's not stupid. She was probably sitting back and plotting how she could cause a scene."

Jenna planted her feet and closed her eyes, shaking her head left to right as she spoke. Had Rumer not witnessed the same scene she had? Did they not watch Dante practically pick another human being up off the floor as if they were a rag doll? "Do you hear yourself? I'm not talking about Ranisha. She was just doing her job, or trying to. All she wanted to do was run the credit card. And what exactly, was wrong with asking a question?" Jenna paused, fuming. "They had a thing, no matter what he told you. She had every right to act surprised, because she really was."

"I don't see what your point is exactly."

"My point is that Dante, your Dante, had no right whatsoever to put his hands on that girl, no matter what she said to him."

"I think you're overreacting." Rumer cocked her head to the side. "I didn't think that was such a big deal."

"Do you hear yourself? He *snatched* her. He lifted her feet off the floor. He's the one that made a series of bad choices beginning with taking us to the place where his 'whatever she is' works." She made air quotes with her fingers. Rumer might as well be blind if she couldn't see that she was about to be in the middle of some terrible mess.

Jenna pleaded with her friend. "We should go. We should leave right now!" Jenna reached for Rumer again, but missed.

"Now who's the crazy one. We can go when Dante comes out." Jenna sighed in exasperation. What was her friend thinking? Was she so into Dante that she couldn't see that this was nothing but a bad situation?

"You're over-reacting!"

"At what?" Dante popped out of the theater and interrupted their discussion. He was back to being all smiles again. Paul, trailing behind him, looked less than happy.

Both girls clammed up, Rumer with her arms crossed over her

chest. Her face flushed and she stood with her back to the wall. "Nothing. Jenna is just being Jenna."

Paul put his hand on her shoulder. "I know how that feels."

Dante laughed. "I don't understand you, man. Can we go?" He made no mention of what had transpired in the movie theater. Jenna and Paul locked eyes now, and butterflies tickled Jenna's stomach, but not because they had a love connection. Something was not quite right, and no one seemed to be able to see it but her.

CHAPTER THIRTEEN

Few words were exchanged between Jenna and Rumer the next morning. When the alarm went off in their dorm room, Rumer silenced it and hopped out of bed. She didn't bother to glance in Jenna's direction, much less wake her. She dressed quickly, with her back turned toward her friend and was purposefully quiet. After last night, she had nothing to say to Jenna and didn't feel like being criticized anymore.

Things had been awkward on the way home. Jenna and Paul had walked ahead, and from what Rumer could tell, they barely spoke to each other. Jenna had looked back over her shoulder a few times, but she never said another word about the Ranisha incident. That had suited Rumer just fine; she was about done with people telling her how to live her life or thinking they knew what was best for her.

She and Dante had taken their time as they walked behind their friends. He'd slipped his arm over her shoulder and pulled her close. Just thinking about it made Rumer shiver. She'd enjoyed the way they fit together perfectly, like two adjacent pieces of a puzzle.

"I'm so sorry about that," he'd said. "I got so caught up. I can't believe that she'd interrupt our date. Truthfully, Ranisha is somewhat of a stalker." Dante had explained everything. Ranisha was an out of control girl with a crush. "We had a couple of classes together. I helped her with her work, and the next thing you know, she's everywhere I turn."

That had been enough for Rumer. Who could blame the girl? she thought. Dante had everything that girls were taught to want in a man. She could see how some girls would be desperate for even a little attention from him. Who wouldn't be? Desperation was not a good look. Too bad that Jenna couldn't see things how she did.

Finally dressed, Rumer turned away from the small mirror in their dorm bathroom, grabbed her bag and headed for the door. Jenna sat straight up in bed. "So you weren't going to wake me?"

"I didn't want to disturb you. You were sleeping so soundly." Rumer cringed. She hated to tell her best friend half-truths.

"That's a load of crap and you know it." She hopped out of bed, her mouth drawn in a frown. "I would never treat you this way. The truth is you didn't want to take the chance that I had anything more to say about last night." Jenna left the bathroom door open so she could talk to Rumer. "Don't worry, I don't. Like you told me last night, you're grown. I will just tell you one last time to be careful, that's all. Now wait for me."

Rumer leaned back against the door to wait for her friend. She would let Jenna command her this morning. She was in too good of a mood to even challenge her on her tone. Jenna might not have anything else to say with her mouth, but her body language would continue to speak loud and clear. She'd never been one to hold her tongue.

Rumer chatted away as they walked across campus, but Jenna was silent. After last night, she didn't have a good feeling about Dante at all, but didn't want to risk making Rumer upset. They slowed as they reached the front of the Student Union. A group of girls blocked their way.

The girls glanced at each other but didn't speak. It was unusual to see so many people outside the Union instead of inside, especially on a day like today. Although it was technically summer, it wasn't particularly warm. In Seattle, the summer weather, especially in August, could be like a flighty girlfriend, and it was chilly at best. They made their way around the crowd and almost walked right into Ranisha and her friends.

Ranisha stood on the bottom step, leaning against the metal railing that lined the steps. She was flanked on either side by the same two friends she'd come into the Union with before. They stopped talking and stared hard at Rumer and Jenna, their mouths set into a thin line. Inside, Rumer shrank back just a little. From the looks of things, they had been the subject of their conversation.

Rumer held her head high, faking confidence. She was not going to be intimidated by Ranisha, in spite of what Dante had shared with her about her stalker tendencies. Instead, she smiled in Ranisha's direction.

Ranisha's eyes were covered by large sunglasses. Rumer couldn't see her eyes, but her lips did not return the smile. Her friends glared at her, so Rumer was sure that Ranisha was glaring, too.

Rumer forced her lips to keep their smile. "Morning, ladies."

She tried her best to walk past them as if they were not staring through her.

Ranisha's two friends let out a collective gasp. Ranisha turned around quickly, facing away from Rumer and Jenna. None of them returned Rumer's greeting, and her friends moved closer together. One of the girls put her arm around Ranisha's shoulder and the other rubbed her back.

Even though she hadn't expected them to answer, Rumer felt like she'd been slapped. That snub was so harsh, it hurt physically. She was determined not to let any of them see that, though. She shrugged and continued up the steps with Jenna by her side. What did she care if these people she didn't know spoke to her?

"That was kind of drama queen like," Jenna tried to whisper, but failed miserably, her voice carrying further than she'd intended.

Ranisha spun back around so fast that her glasses flew off her face and skidded across the ground. "You think you're all that?" she growled.

Jenna, Rumer and Ranisha's friends froze in place.

She continued. "In a few weeks, you'll be me. You just wait. He'll be done with you and then he'll throw you away like a piece of trash." Her voice was shaky and much higher than normal, but quickly became lost in her friends' replies of "Don't do it, girl," and "She's not worth it."

No one spoke. A few other people turned around to see where the commotion had come from. Ranisha's friend grabbed the glasses that had flown off of Ranisha's face and extended them to her.

People stared openly and Rumer's eyes followed the glasses from the ground, then watched as Ranisha's friend slowly walked toward her. Her eyes widened at what she saw.

A whisper went through the crowd. Ranisha's face was all but bashed in, covered in black bruises all throughout her eye area. It looked as if she'd fallen on her head and now had internal bleeding around her eye sockets. Rumer gasped.

It was Ranisha's turn to hold her head up. She tossed her hair, and then slowly and deliberately put her glasses back on her face. Her friends formed a human fortress together and they walked away from the Student Union together.

"Wow." Jenna looked in the direction they'd gone.

"What was that about?" Rumer asked.

"You can't be so naïve. You're kidding me, right?" Jenna looked at her friend in disbelief. Had they not witnessed the same thing?

"What do you mean?"

"Please don't tell me that you didn't see her face."

"No," Rumer said. "I saw it. What do you think happened?" Rumer swallowed hard. "That looked terrible. Her eye was purple."

Jenna didn't want to spell it out, but it looked like she was going to have to. "I hope I'm wrong, but it looks like she was beat up, and I bet I can guess who did it."

"No way, Jenna. Don't be ridiculous. I think it's unfair of you to jump to conclusions."

"I'm not jumping to anything. I think you should check your boyfriend's hands, though. Bruises like that almost always go both ways."

Rumer didn't get to see Dante. He wasn't running on the track and he was nowhere to be found in the science buildings. She'd hoped to run into him before lab, but that didn't happen. She kept finding excuses to go to the bathroom, hoping she would see him, but by mid-afternoon, her mood was trashed. This was the one day of the week that there was no lecture happening, so she couldn't even look forward to that. Jenna seemed to read her mind.

"Looking for your man?" The Union was more quiet in the afternoon than it was in the morning. They walked in together, and there were only a few students milling around or sitting at the tables with their heads deep into books.

Rumer pursed her lips and counted to ten. ...*seven, eight, nine*... "Are we gonna fight? Because I am not in the mood." Jenna had no idea how close she was to getting cussed out. "And you can stop looking at me with that I-told-you-so look on your face."

Jenna's face said everything. "I don't know what you mean, but I can tell that you're wondering where the hell Dante is, now that you saw his *girlfriend* all beat up. I get it. I'd be trying to make sense of things, too."

"Do you always have to try and analyze things? Why can't things just be as they are? Why can't it just be that I'm tired from hanging out late and then staying up to get my stuff done?" Sometimes, Jenna had a way of getting on her last nerve, especially when she had to beat a point into the ground.

Amusement danced on Jenna's face. "Just calm down. I haven't said any of that. Goodness. What happened to being able to take a little teasing? Isn't that what we do?" She sighed. "Don't be made at me because I recognize your man's game."

"You don't know what you're talking about."

"I don't?" Jenna took a deep breath in and wet her lips. "He doesn't care about you. If he did, he would have made sure you were in to take care of your business. You are way too smart not to realize that are just a pawn."

Rumer shrugged. "Not everything is a conspiracy theory."

"If you say so. I'm done talking."

"I doubt that." Rumer spit out her reply.

Jenna's face darkened. She was only trying to help. "I really don't like how you treat me like all of this is my fault. I have nothing to do with you being impatient. I have nothing to do with how your bad boy treats you or any of the other women in his life." Her voice had slowly escalated from a normal speaking level to just below a yell. A few people glanced in their direction.

Rumer looked around the room to see who was watching. Her face was hot. Most looked away. She could feel their eyes on her. *Now who was being unreasonable*, she thought. "Can you keep it down?"

"I can. But you do realize what this is, don't you?" Her voice had lowered to a very loud hiss. "It's the bad boy syndrome."

Rumer pressed her lips together in disbelief. *What was Jenna spouting off about now?* "The bad boy syndrome? Did you Google that last night or something?" She had more to say, but a flash from her phone caught her eye. "You're not," she flipped it over to read her text message, "a psychologist." Her voice trailed off. The message was from Dante. Her lips curled into a smile. Distracted now, she typed a message in a flurry of thumb activity.

"Let me guess. That's him. He's texting to tell you he misses you and will see you shortly." She pursed her lips.

Rumer didn't reply as she corrected her message. There was nothing friendly or warm about the near smile that rested on her face.

"No, wait, he's asking you out."

Rumer's phone flashed again almost immediately. She answered so fast she almost dropped her phone. What did Jenna know about it, anyway? She didn't have a man. Not that she did. Dante was sort of her man, right?

Jenna continued. "Classic. It really is. Good, clean-cut girl, attracted to the guy that walks the bad boy line? He's slightly dangerous, pitting one woman against the other. He's older, in a position of authority, but he's skirting the rules."

"You read too much romance." Rumer busied herself with her phone. By now, she was smiling ear to ear.

"I read just enough to recognize a bad romance when I see it." Jenna waited while Rumer finished texting. By now, she was in so deep that she doubted that her friend could even hear anything she was saying. After a few minutes, she cleared her throat. "Well, I think I'm going to go." She pushed out her chair. "There's no use in me staying around if I'm going to be ignored. There are better things I could be doing with my time."

Rumer looked up, finally placing her phone on the table. "Wait, wait, wait. I'm sorry. I'm done." She pushed the phone away from her. "What were you saying?"

Jenna shook her head slowly. "Nothing." Hadn't she heard anything? "So, when are you meeting him?"

Rumer glanced at the time on her phone, her eyes downcast. "In an hour."

Jenna's face fell. "So, I guess we aren't studying tonight. Remember that thing we do?" They'd planned to do review later that evening. It was something they'd done every other day since the summer started.

"Oh, right." She looked around as if she were lost. "I'll make it up to you."

"I really didn't think this was about me. Just be careful, Rumer. I'm going to go." She stacked her things to make them easier to carry. "You just be careful. Even good swimmers can get caught in the undertow. I'll talk to you later."

"What? Why you gotta be that way? And why do you have to walk around sounding like a walking advice blog?"

Jenna's eyes bore a hole through her friend. "What way? Sensible?" She shrugged, speaking over her shoulder as she walked away. "It's like talking to a brick wall."

CHAPTER FOURTEEN

"Bam!" Dante said, slamming his phone down on the table like a winning domino. He folded his arms across his chest and leaned back on the wall in his apartment.

Tyrone's mouth dropped open. "What? No way!" he said.

"Yes, way. It's done. Rumer is coming over here."

"Whooooaaa!" Tyrone practically yelled. "You are way too smooth for your own good. I want to know how you do that. One minute, you don't know their last name. Next minute, she's in your bed, just like that."

"Wait, what is her last name?" They broke into laughter.

Paul walked into the room, acting as if he hadn't overheard his friends. "What's all the commotion? Just like what?"

Tyrone was practically jumping up and down. "Dante—"

Dante cut him off. "Nothing man. The usual stuff. You know our boy here is all *over* eager about everything."

Paul narrowed his eyes. "Maybe he is a little enthusiastic, but he usually has a reason for his," he paused. "Exuberance."

"Call it what you want. Dante is a boss, though." Tyrone shuffled back and forth from foot to foot. "He has a date that requires us to vacate our space for a bit."

"Oh?" Paul waited. Tyrone would tell him everything if he just gave him room to.

He didn't have to wait long. Tyrone was like a five-year-old that could barely contain himself. "Oh, yeah. He's got Rumer coming over later. You know what *that* means."

Unfortunately, he did know. There had been too many times when Dante had just been not nice to the women he dated, and the women were the ones that ended up hurt. He was all for fun, but he was getting tired of picking up the pieces, and Dante was skirting the rules where Rumer was concerned. Paul spun around. "Really, Dante?" His face was filled with disgust. "She's a nice girl. Don't forget that."

"You need to stay out of my business. Since when are you such a saint? You never had anything to say about my lady friends and how I handled them before."

"Therein lies the problem. You don't treat women like they have feelings. According to you, they all have to be 'handled'. You're a caveman." Paul paused, lowering his voice. "You went too far last night."

"Whatever, man. You just don't understand. Why're you worried now? You need to be worried about your own stuff. You could be hooking up with Jenna. She ain't bad looking. Want me to tell Rumer that she should come, too?"

Paul just stared at his friend. Dante was missing the point. "Tyrone thinks you're all that, but you really are clueless."

"What? What's wrong with you? You don't like women

126

anymore?"

Paul drew back his fist to hit Dante, but then stopped himself. There was no way he was going to let himself be baited into a bad situation by Dante, again.

"Uh huh. I know you ain't crazy." Dante clenched and reopened his fists.

Calmer now, Paul continued. "Leave it to you to take it there when you feel threatened. I *should* have said something before." He paused, licking his lips as he tried to compose himself further. Wasn't Dante supposedly the smart one among them? "The way you treat women is despicable. How would you feel if one of these people were your sister? Or your mother?"

"You can leave my mother out of this. Just be gone at seven. You're not normal, Paul. This is what men our age are supposed to be doing. I don't have time to argue with you."

"*Men* treat people with respect." Paul paused to let that sink in even though he doubted he was getting anywhere. "No argument here." He held his hands up, palms open in surrender. His nostrils flared. "I absolutely hope you have one helluva date."

CHAPTER FIFTEEN

There was nothing in her closet. Rumer had dug around for the past twenty minutes, unsure of what she should wear to go out with Dante. It had to be right, she didn't want to do too much, and it had to be dual purpose. Her mother would see her first and it had to be acceptable to her, too.

Jenna held up a skirt she found in the bottom of her bag. Rumer studied it, then shook her head. "Girl, this is just too short. Can't you hear my mother now?"

"Yeah, Alma would kind of trip on this. It would hug your hips and show your legs off."

"Yes, and that's the problem. You know how she is. She'll be asking me if I'm going to work on the corner. It's cute, though."

Jenna agreed. "She is really old-fashioned."

"I prefer conservative."

"Too bad we don't have a burka. You could wear that and put your real outfit underneath it."

The girls broke into laughter at the suggestion, but Rumer was not above changing like she'd done in middle school. She finally settled on a tight-fitted pair of jeans and a cute top. Jenna handed her a pair of heels. "Wear these. This will do it."

Rumer held them in her hands. "But you love these."

"I do. But I can't have my girl out there looking crazy."

As she slipped them on her feet, Rumer held onto the bed, teetering on the four-inch heels. "These shoes are the truth. And I'll certainly be hot. Won't be able to run anywhere, either."

"You got this." Jenna smiled. "It's not like you're trying to run, anyway."

"I know that's right." Rumer paused. "Wait, are you being sarcastic?"

Jenna shrugged, but said nothing.

A knock on the door caused them both to jump. Rumer clutched her chest. They looked at each other quizzically, and Jenna laughed over her shoulder as she opened the door. "I wasn't expecting—"

Paul stood outside the door with a sheepish look on his face. "I hope you don't mind my stopping by."

"Um…" Jenna stuttered and Rumer was frozen in place.

"Aren't you going to invite me in?" He leaned on the doorjamb and peered around Jenna.

"Rumer is getting dressed."

"Oh," he said. "I'm sorry. I didn't mean to intrude. I'll just—"

"No," Rumer said. "I'm decent. It's fine." She raised her eyebrows at Jenna.

Jenna stepped aside to let Paul enter. "I wasn't expecting you."

"I know. I was just thinking about you." He looked at Rumer. "You look nice, Rumer."

A warm feeling coursed through Rumer's body, and she

blushed. "Thanks. I'm just going to dinner at my mother's. It's our thing."

"I see."

"And she's going out with Dante after!"

Rumer glared at her friend. Did she have to tell everything? "Not a big deal. We're just going to hang out some."

Paul nodded. "Okay. That's what's up. As good as you look…" He walked around Rumer so he could see all sides of her.

"For real, Paul?" Jenna glared at him, crossing her arms.

"I have to give credit where credit is due." He put his arm around Jenna's shoulder. "That takes nothing from you, Jenna." Jenna visibly relaxed, satisfied. "So, where are you going?"

Rumer shrugged. "Dunno. It's a not a big deal. Everyone has a lot of work to do tonight."

"True that. Well, you be careful, okay?" Jenna said.

"Careful? He doesn't bite." Paul laughed.

Paul laughed. "You never know what can happen. As good as you look, a brother might not be able to control himself."

"You make Dante sound like a Neanderthal. I thought he was your friend."

"He is. We've been friends a long time. I know him better than most people." He turned to Jenna. "That's not why I came, though. I was going to see if you wanted to hang out, but I can settle for just one half of the duo. You feel like getting some coffee, Jenna?"

Jenna's nod was slow. "I guess I can do something. We're still meeting at midnight to work on our stuff, right, Rumer?"

"That's the plan. You have a good time."

Paul walked to the door, and Jenna leaned in to whisper to her friend. "Don't let all that go to your head. You know it's my shoes that make your outfit all that." She winked.

Rumer laughed a little, but she knew that Jenna was half-serious. She waited for them to leave, and then turned to the mirror to admire her reflection. She did look good. She loved the way her jeans made her behind look. Although her shirt was really just a tee shirt, it hugged her in all the right places so that her abs showed through. *Who could resist this?*

She checked her lipstick, thinking about Paul and his comments. Why did people keep warning her about Dante? He was cool, not to mention sexy. Whatever was in his past was in his past. She admired herself again, then checked her watch. She was going to have to run. Could it be that they were just haters?

CHAPTER SIXTEEN

The bus was entirely too slow but Rumer couldn't afford an Uber. She glanced at the time on her phone. Even though they were in the High Occupancy Lane, they were moving slowly, barely above a crawl. She sighed. She could probably walk faster. No driving skill at all must be required to be a bus driver, she thought. She fidgeted in her seat. Didn't he know she had a hot date?

The time crunch was simple. She'd completely forgotten that she was supposed to go see her mother today. For one hot second, she'd thought about just calling her mother and telling her that she couldn't come to dinner, that she was just too busy, but that thought went away just as quickly as it had arrived. If she didn't show up, all hell would break loose. As it was, she'd have less than an hour to hang around before she'd have to get dressed to hang out with Dante. Lucky for her, he'd agreed to come pick her up so she wouldn't have to take the bus back to the University area. The down side of that was she'd have to answer all kinds of questions from her mother. That woman could interrogate a person better than the CIA, and this was one opportunity Rumer knew she wouldn't miss.

The idea of Dante meeting her mother scared her. If he picked her up, that meant no matter how much she envisioned herself slipping out of the house when her mother wasn't looking, it would be impossible. Rumer knew this all the way down to her toes that there was no way on God's green earth that Alma was letting that happen. There was not much that took place on their street her mother didn't know about. She'd probably invite Dante in, give him a drink, and then grill him about his ancestry and his plans for the future.

Alma would want to know everything about him, down to what he wanted to name his firstborn. Hopefully, the grand interrogation wouldn't take up too much of their date time. Rumer had no doubt that her mother would uncover any secret that Dante even thought he had, all the way back to his great grandfather's middle name, in about ten minutes. Certainly not ideal, but Rumer could think of no way around it.

By the time the bus finally reached the corner of her block, Rumer was ready to run. How was she going to make her mother happy enough for her to be comfortable with her going on a date with some guy she'd never met on their dinner night? She was in a weird place. Technically, she was still in high school, but mature enough for her mother to trust her on a college campus alone for six weeks. No matter how old she was, though, her mother wouldn't be changing her opinions any time soon.

Rumer really had no idea how her mother was going to react. It would most likely be a toss-up between "It's about time" and "That's not what I sent you there for." As much as her mother was old-fashioned and wanted her to date and get married and all that, she wanted her daughter to be self-sufficient and independent.

Rumer practically flew down the street and let herself into the house. The only thing worse than not showing up would be to show up late, and now she'd added all types of complications to the mix. Her stomach was in jumbles as she tried to make sense of it all.

"Hey, baby? How are you?" Her mother called to her from the kitchen as soon as she opened the door. She used the voice she reserved for Rumer, appearing from the depths of her house, so soundlessly that it was as if she'd materialized out of nowhere. Despite her nervousness, Rumer smiled. A pang of homesickness hit her. Her mother was wearing almost exactly what she had been when Rumer saw her last, when she'd dropped her off on campus. Her fashionable sweats were covered with an apron and she had flour from head to toe. She was a diva, but was absolutely old-fashioned at the same time. One of her favorite things to do was to bake, and from the looks of things, she was hard at work.

"Hey, Mom. What are you making today?" Rumer inhaled, trying to identify the smells that were greeting her at the door.

"Only your favorites. You know how I do when my *favorite* Rumer comes home."

Rumer couldn't help but smile. She acted as if Rumer had been gone months rather than just a few weeks. "Mom, I'm your *only* Rumer." The reply was the same as it had been for as long as Rumer could remember. It was corny, but no matter how many times her mother called her that, Rumer felt safe. She relaxed just some, her shoulders dropping down a little as the tension flowed from her body. Her mother had that effect on her. As anxious as she made her, she relaxed her, too.

"You shouldn't have cooked, though. I can't stay long."

Powerless to resist, Rumer let her mother wrap herself around her. "Nonsense. Who would I be if I didn't cook for my heart? Gimme a hug and come on in here." Her mother wrapped her arms around her daughter and paused. Rumer sank in, enjoying the familiar scent of old-fashioned baby powder mixed with Chanel 19.

"Your father would be so proud." Her mother's voice cracked, and Rumer froze. "God rest his soul."

Would he be proud? she thought. She loved her mother, revisionist history and all. Although she couldn't remember much about her father, Rumer knew not to say anything. She'd long accepted the fact that it was better for her mother to remember the positive things about the man that had donated his sperm to her creation. He'd died of a heart attack twelve years ago, but Rumer didn't remember him being proud of her or kind to her mother at all. What she did remember were harsh words, bruises and crying, and her mother's cover-ups and excuses for him. She also remembered her mother getting so many beatings from him that she almost took the idea of being ride or die for your man, literally.

Rumer had tried to talk to her about it once, but the answer she got hadn't made sense. "Sometimes, women have to sacrifice to keep the man they love in their lives. We have to be patient, even if it's not pleasant."

She tried to release herself from her mother's embrace,

remembering that her mother's idea of sacrifice had included three broken ribs and a crushed eye socket. Her right eye still looked somehow different from the other, but her mother mourned her father to this day like he'd been the greatest husband ever created. Maybe he was, but Rumer had yet to understand love like that.

"I have a date, Mom. I hate to eat and run." Her voice trailed off. She didn't think it was going to fly, but it was worth a try.

"I don't understand what that means, Rumer." Alma's mouth was drawn into a thin line. That is what her mother did, she would just refuse to comprehend anything that wasn't the way she liked it to be, and Rumer not having dinner with her or cutting their time short certainly was not to her liking. Alma grabbed plates and started setting the table for two as she always did, ignoring what Rumer's words.

Rumer let out a heavy sigh. She might as well have just told her the sun was shining outside. Her mother hadn't even paused. This was a game she could not win. "Okay. Let's set an extra place. We're going to have company." She watched as her mother's body language did a complete 360.

Rumer leaving was not acceptable news, but having company was something she could live with. Entertaining was one of her mother's favorite things. All through high school, she'd continually goaded Rumer, wanting their house to be the one where the kids hung out. She loved being surrounded by people.

"If you and your friends are here," she'd say, "I won't have to track you down in the street when I need you." Rumer planned to use that to her advantage today. She held her breath, hoping that she had her mother pegged like she thought she did.

"That's good. I knew something was going on since you came in here looking so fancy. If your jeans were any tighter they would be painted on." She gave her daughter a knowing look. "I always enjoy company. And I cooked enough for an army."

Rumer chuckled. Next, the questions would start. She might as well just go with it. "Of course you did, Mom." There was no use in being upset about things. If she were pleasant, they would be done faster and she might avoid a lecture, although she cringed a bit at the idea that her mother would undoubtedly interrogate Dante to death. She fired off a text, hoping it wouldn't scare him off.

Hey, hope you don't mind having a few bites to eat before we go. My mother is way overprotective. It will make things a little easier and you don't have to stay long. And I promise she doesn't bite. Often.

Rumer held her breath while she waited. Either Dante would reply, or he wouldn't. This would give her a chance to see what he was actually made of. She winced at the thought, not sure that she was ready to actually know. If he didn't show up, that could be a problem. That would be all she needed. She'd already told her mother he was coming, so if he didn't show, that would be a disaster. Then she'd be the one stuck answering questions all night.

She didn't have to wait long.

NP. On the way.

His reply made her even more nervous. No problem? What did that mean? Texts were impossible to decipher. Was it really no problem, or was it that he was already on his way so he might as well keep coming? She bit her lip, pulling the skin from it with her teeth. Those were two very different things.

"What time is your friend coming?" her mother asked. "You know I don't like the food to get cold and it's going to be ready in exactly seven minutes."

The last three words echoed in Rumer's head. Unless he was around the corner, there was no way Dante would show up in seven minutes. And Seattle traffic was pure hell. If the bus couldn't get through, how would one guy in an ordinary car? Was she setting him up for failure before things even got started? Maybe inviting him was not such a good idea. If things with Dante and her mother got off to a bad start, their date, which she was really looking forward to, could go downhill fast.

Twenty minutes later, the doorbell rang. Rumer's stomach did a backflip. She hoped that Dante would take her up on the dinner offer, but hadn't expected him to arrive that quickly, as on time as he could be, given the short notice. True to form, her mother would start dinner with or without everyone present, and Rumer had managed to stall her long enough that they were just about ready to sit down to dinner. Alma was still in the kitchen, checking on the food once again.

Her mother looked at her quizzically, as if they hadn't had a discussion about an extra person at dinner. "I'll get it, Mom. It's my friend, remember."

Alma kept stirring the pot, nodding. "I suppose your friend has a name?" She pursed her lips, not taking her eyes off the contents of her   pot.

Rumer wasn't sure what her mother's reluctance was really about, but she was used to her being a wild card. Anything could set her off at any given time. Did her mother not want to share her or something? "Um, yes, he does, Mom. I told you, remember? Dante?" This was going to be more difficult than she'd imagined. She clenched her teeth, silently counting to ten. Her mother was already being passive-aggressive.

She wiped her hands on the old-fashioned apron that now covered her sweats, then reached around to remove it. "Well, go get him. It's time to eat."

Breathing hard, Rumer opened the door to let him in. Butterflies danced in her stomach, and she tried to shake them off. On a normal day, she was a rational person. Rumer thought back to a few days ago, when she was supposed to have been in control of this journey, of creating the new person that everyone wanted to be around. Dante had somehow managed to make an illusion of control fly out of her head inside of a week. Rumer flushed.

He winked. "Hey, thank you for the invitation, Mrs. Johnson. So nice to see that the apple didn't fall far from the tree." Dante turned it on hard, and Rumer gushed. He was hot, but she had no idea he had this effect on everyone, but she was glad he did. In the blink of an eye, Alma went from reluctant to practically melting in his hands.

Rumer felt silly for worrying so hard. Dante clearly had this, too.

Was there anything that he wasn't good at? This might not be so bad after all.

CHAPTER SEVENTEEN

Rumer waved goody-bye to her mother as they pulled away from the curb. Their stomachs were full and her body was on high alert from the excitement and anticipation of Dante actually coming to her house, meeting her mother, and then having it go well. The whole thing had gone better than she could have ever imagined.

She'd never really brought a boy home before, at least, not where she presented him as her date. And inviting one to dinner, well, before a few weeks ago, Rumer would have never thought to do that. Most times, it was just best not to give her mother an opportunity to be in the middle of the few almost-relationships that she'd had, and that had been a good thing. The one time she'd even come close, the whole thing had ended in a triangle disaster with Rumer being on the losing corner.

Rumer didn't know what to think about this afternoon. She felt like a spectator in some huge production as she watched Dante work his magic, practically reducing her mother to a giggling teenaged girl. He'd headed off the barrage of questions masterfully, instead making her mother the focus of the discussion. They never even spoke about how old he was. Rumer had thought sure that that one would be a problem for her mother, but Dante had sidestepped around how they'd met so skillfully, Rumer was left both amazed and just a little jealous.

From the moment he'd stepped through the door, Dante had turned the charm on hard, and her mother was suddenly a person that she could barely recognize. The dinner went from being Rumer's dinner, to Dante being the center of attention. He was so charming, Rumer was almost convinced that he'd actually been flirting with Alma.

"I think that went well," he said.

"You think?" She almost didn't want to tell him that he had no idea of the miracle he'd just worked. "I think my mother now has the hots for you."

"C'mon. I was just being a gentleman, and I knew you were uncomfortable. I wanted to make you happy."

"Is that what you call it?" She looked out the side window, her head turned away from Dante. She needed to make sense of what she was feeling before she said anything else. On one hand, she was glad that the dinner had gone far better than she would have ever hoped, but on the less rational side, she'd felt as if he'd turned it on just a little too thick.

Dante put his hand on her thigh near her knee and squeezed it gently. "Your mother is a smart woman."

Rumer's heart jumped a little, and she cursed herself for being so easy to cave. A flood of warmth spread through her, starting from the place his hand rested on her leg. She stared at it. Why did Dante have to be so irresistible? "Not so smart that she wasn't bowled over by your charm. She never saw you coming, that's for sure."

"She could tell that I only have eyes for one woman right now." He smiled, training his huge, expressive eyes on hers. "And I was just doing what I've been raised to do. If nothing else, I know how to make a woman happy, even your mother. If she's not happy, you won't be, either."

Ain't that the truth, Rumer thought. "She does have a way of making everyone miserable if she doesn't think things are the way they should be. I thought she'd be more difficult, though."

"The only thing that matters is you and me. And this little gathering I found for us to go to." He leaned to the side, driving with one hand.

"Gathering?" They hadn't really talked about what they were going to do in their date. Rumer had been so glad that he'd asked, she just said yes without any further questions. "Don't forget I have some work to get done."

"Don't worry about that. You'll have plenty of time to get your stuff in. I got you."

"You got me?" Confusion was beginning to be a familiar feeling, but it was nice thought. As soon as she thought it, she felt a pang of guilt. She never wanted to be the kind of student who got her grades any other way than having earned them, but it might be nice not to have to work so hard all the time.

"Yes," he said. "I'll make sure that you have what you need."

"I hope you're not implying that I'm going to get any special treatment, Professor."

"You can save the terms of endearment for later." Dante's eyes twinkled. "I promise you won't get any special treatment. At least not in the classroom."

Rumer wasn't sure she was satisfied, and felt a little uneasy. She wanted to do well in the class, but because she did well in the class, not because she went on a few dates with the temporary professor. She nodded anyway.

"So, are you game or what?" He looked at her too long to be in a moving car.

"Of course I am." Rumer blushed. It felt good that he wanted to give her so much attention. He had a lot of girls to choose from, including those like Ranisha. Besides her bad attitude, she was gorgeous. All of his friends seemed to be so much more together than Rumer felt. She might as well enjoy it before he figured out her real truth; that she was only playacting. It was amazing that Dante wanted to be with her at all, really. There was no way that she was passing on the opportunity, especially after he'd gone out of his way to charm her mother. Rumer beat down the familiar feeling of insecurity that was growing inside her. He was here, wasn't he? If hanging out a few hours was going to make him happy, she had no intention of denying him that.

"Are you embarrassed?" Dante looked at her incredulously. "That's sweet. That's one of the things I like about you, Rumer."

Her heart skipped a beat. She shook her head. "I'm tougher than that." He'd said *one* of the things, and that implied that there were more things that he liked.

"That's what I thought."

"We can go, but I do need to be back to campus," she paused, not wanting to sound like a baby. "By maybe, midnight?" If she had to, she'd stay up all night to get her work done, and Jenna could start on the project without her. She cringed just a little, feeling guilty that she'd even thought that. Jenna wouldn't like it and would probably make her pay for it for a while, but Dante was worth it.

"You're the boss."

They pulled into the driveway of the Hyatt and the car was immediately flanked by the valet parking people.

"You didn't say we were going to a hotel." Rumer hesitated. There was a part of her that felt as if it might not be a great idea to be at a hotel with Dante, but she trusted him. "This is fancy."

Dante chuckled, handing his car keys to the parking attendant. "I didn't think it mattered. There are a few of us that hang out here. It's sort of become the spot. When football season is in, a lot of the players come here and it gets taken over, so we enjoy it while we can. It's easy to get in and out of and no one asks too many questions."

They met near the front of the car, and Dante immediately took her hand in his. "This is okay, isn't it?"

She nodded. It was more than okay. From the moment her hand interlocked with his, Rumer felt somehow older and more sophisticated. She stood up straight as they walked toward the front entrance of the building, adopting that walk she perfected, the one that said, "Look at me," only this time, she believed it. Being with Dante had somewhat transformed her and she didn't have to fake her confidence. She let him guide her through the revolving door and into the brightly-lit lobby.

For a weeknight, it was teeming with people. The lobby flowed right into the bar, a wide open space with comfortable seating all over, placed in groups of four or six. Rumer recognized several people from the party the other night.

The room seemed to stop when they entered. Normally, a situation where everyone stopped in their tracks would make Rumer feel like she wanted to run and hide, and she probably did hesitate just a little, but Dante sensed her reluctance and pulled her forward. They were barely through the door and he was practically shouting his hellos. A few people walked in their direction.

"You know everyone," she whispered, talking more to herself than to Dante, but he heard anyway and looked over his shoulder.

He winked at her and took a sip of the drink he'd been handed. His gaze comforted Rumer just enough for her to notice the low music playing in the room. It filled in the gaps in the conversations, making the low murmurs seem more like a roar. Rumer tried to scan the area around her. She had no idea that this hotel that she'd been past so many times had another life that she'd never imagined. As far as she knew, it was just a place for conferences and maybe the occasional fancy Sunday brunch, not a hangout for the "it" crowd. Now it seemed so much more interesting than it had before.

The room had a life of its own. Dante greeted his friends and even talked to some people he didn't know. Rumer watched in amazement, admiring his comfort. They were somehow drawn into the middle of the crowd and Dante slapped people on the back and laughed every other minute, in between, stopping and exchanging man-hugs with people he seemed to know well.

Was there anyone he didn't know? Rumer didn't spot one person she knew by name, but most of the people gave Rumer, at the very least, a nod. A few others hugged her like they were old friends. How many of the people would even give her the time of day if she saw them anywhere else, like on campus? she wondered. Dante had held her hand and she'd stepped into some world that hadn't been visible to her before, like in a fairy tale. She smiled. Rumer had no idea how long this might last, but right now, she wanted to bask in the glow of Dante's light, enjoying what popular felt like. Never in her life had she been treated as part of the in-crowd like this.

"Is it always like this or is this a special occasion?"

"You're going to have to get used to this if you're going to hang with me," Dante said. "This is how it is. I've kind of been around awhile and I do have a lot of friends. I'm popular. It's what people expect."

That's something I would know nothing about, Rumer thought. Did he always do what people expected? If that was the case, then they weren't much different. Maybe that was what she sensed that first day she'd seen him. They were kindred spirits.

Rumer wasn't superstitious or anything like that, but what if they were meant to be?

Her palms were starting to sweat. Dante was getting too much attention. In just a few hours, she'd learned so much about him and had a ton of questions, but this wasn't the place to ask them. She didn't want to start a discussion that would be impossible to finish with all of the people that were around. She was just glad to be with him, but it looked like all of these other people were, too. It was a type of attention she had no experience with at all.

He worked the crowd with the ease of someone who knew what they wanted and was in control of his life, another something that was alien to Rumer, but he had a way of making her feel included anyway. They weren't exactly having an intimate night, but he wasn't leaving here behind, either. It felt good to be next to Dante, but she wasn't sure which she would prefer.

Dante kept her close for most of the few minutes that they were in the lobby. He made sure that everyone knew that they were together, and Rumer really appreciated that. Her smile was plastered to her face, and she tried her best to look like she was comfortable, but the butterflies in her stomach threatened to betray her.

Rumer soon figured out the music she was hearing was actually coming from a small nightclub in the rear of the lobby. A feeling of dread hit her in the pit of her stomach. Is that where they were ultimately headed? She made a note to herself to ask more questions next time. That was the only way she was going to know what to expect.

They got closer to that corner every minute as Dante worked the crowd. Did he remember that she wasn't yet twenty-one? A thousand questions ran through her mind. She would melt through the floor if they carded her. Her face blanched and she struggled to keep her smile in place. She didn't even own a decent fake ID.

Rumer became lost in her thoughts of worry, and soon, all she could hear around her were the Charlie Brown sounds of Dante talking to the other people in the lobby. A hand on her wrist drove her back to the present. She gasped and looked up and her eyes met Paul's.

"Hey, Rumer," he said. "You good?" He smiled at her warmly. If they hadn't started out so poorly, Rumer realized that she might even like him.

She nodded, licking her lips. "How are you?"

"Me? I'm fine." His voice was so low, it seemed to slide underneath the din of the room. "You look kind of pale. I didn't realize that this is where you were going when I saw you earlier."

Dante's back was turned toward them, laughing at his discussion with two guys on his other side. He spun around quickly, locking eyes with Paul. "Paul. How's it going? I see you made it out tonight." There was no sign of the laughter that had been on his face just a few seconds before, and the tone of his words made Rumer feel as if there was some sub-context to their exchange that she was not privy to.

Paul lifted his chin in greeting. "Hey, yeah, what's up, Dante? I thought that you'd be at your apartment tonight, studying or some shit like that."

Rumer frowned. Paul already knew that wasn't true.

"Rumer and I plan on ending there a little later." He wrapped his arms around her waist, pulling her closer. "Even smart people have a little fun sometimes. We're just swinging through to check things out."

"I hear you," Paul said. "So, I'll see the two of you inside Chances, then?"

"Yeah, man." They gripped palms and then locked arms in a familiar man embrace. Rumer nodded, then faked a smile, staring ahead in the direction of the lounge.

The doors of Chances gaped open at the back of the room, beckoning to Rumer, calling her as if it were a black hole that she was going to be sucked inside if they got too close. Her stomach was twisted in knots. She caught a glimpse of Ranisha's friends from the corner of her eyes. Was it her imagination or were all of them staring?

She looked around quickly, but didn't see Ranisha. Dante was unconcerned and worked the room oblivious to the attention they were getting. Someone said something to her that she was too distracted to get. She nodded and smiled, preoccupied.

Rumer was embarrassed in advance at the idea of being denied entry to the club in front of everybody who was anybody. If that happened, her days of being in the "in" group would be over before they'd begun, and she would once again be an outcast, labeled forever as the baby that couldn't get into club, the one that had drawn unnecessary attention to the good thing they all had going on at the Hyatt. The place loomed larger and larger as they got closer.

"You good?" Dante looked at Rumer, his face full of questions.

Rumer nodded too quickly.

Dante gripped her hand tighter. Could he read her thoughts? "Don't worry. It'll be fine," he said. "Trust me."

She wanted to trust him, but the nagging in her stomach was hard to ignore. Was she just supposed to take it for granted that whoever was checking IDs was going to look her in the face and decide that she was far enough past twenty-one that he could just wave her in?

Finally, they made it to the door. Rumer tried to shrink herself behind Dante.

He laughed. "What are you doing? He won't bite you."

"Are you sure of that?"

"Don't let his size fool you. Damon is a pussycat."

"You know him?" Rumer relaxed just a little.

"Oh, yeah," Dante said. "He went to high school with my brother. We're cool." Dante unleashed his smile again. "I told you, I got this."

Finally, it was their turn. The bouncer made eye contact with Dante and almost smiled. "Hey, what's up, man? Good to see you back."

He glanced down at Rumer. "Who's this?"

If Rumer didn't know better, she would think that he had just given her a disapproving look. She stood up straighter and tried to look more mature. She tried to act as if their conversation didn't matter.

Dante looked at her and smiled. "This is my girl." He said it was such authority that no one would dare question him.

Rumer blushed. *Did he just say that I was his girl?* she thought. How had that happened? It didn't matter how. She liked the sound of it.

CHAPTER EIGHTEEN

The inside of Chances was more crowded than the lobby. From just a few feet inside the door, people were packed so tightly that Rumer felt trapped. If she'd been uncomfortable before, she felt really out of place now. She held tightly onto Dante's hand, trailing behind him as they made their way across the room. The jazz that had sounded soft from the lobby was too loud to talk now. The music enveloped them, and although there wasn't enough room to dance, everyone swayed slightly to the rhythm that filled the room.

They stopped near a set of tables and Dante jerked Rumer's hand up. Before she could protest, he cut the plastic bracelet the bouncer had fastened to her wrist and slipped it in his pocket. They locked eyes and he winked, then nodded. They smiled together at their shared secret. The bouncer hadn't embarrassed her as Rumer thought he might. He hadn't even asked for ID. He'd made no fuss over her age and had fastened the bracelet that indicated her age so quickly, no one had noticed.

"You won't be needing that," he said.

Rumer rubbed her arm. She was glad he'd removed it. Her arms were uncovered and the bright yellow bracelet had advertised its presence, practically glowing in the dark and made her feel even more out of place. Dante put his face so close to hers that Rumer could feel his breath on her cheek. Her stomach tickled as he softly pressed his lips to her check.

"You're beautiful," he said in her ear.

Rumer blushed. What do you say to that? A waitress pushed her way through the crowd and Dante grabbed her arm as she passed, stopping her.

"Bring me two shots of Fireball."

The waitress nodded and scribbled on her pad, then disappeared back into the crowd.

"Thirsty?"

"One's for you."

Rumer's breath caught in her throat. She didn't even know what a Fireball was, but she wasn't about to tell Dante that.

"You okay with that?"

Rumer inhaled, taking in Dante's scent. She was okay with anything he brought forward. "I'm good."

He pulled her close, pressing his body to hers. He swayed and Rumer followed, nestling her face in the crook of his neck. His closeness made her dizzy and she held onto him for balance, feeling as if she might fall off a cliff if she let go.

Rumer hadn't imagined being this close to Dante, so she had no idea it could feel like this. Although the room was packed, it was as if they were the only two there, and everyone else faded back into the background. Dante's closeness put her in a trancelike state and she felt like she was suspended in air.

He pulled away from Rumer like a Band-Aid ripped from a wound. She gasped. It took her a second to realize that the waitress had returned. She sat two shot glasses down on the nearby table, squatting slightly so that her tray didn't dip and nothing was revealed underneath her very tiny skirt.

Dante barely looked in the woman's direction, instead slipping his debit card onto the round tray the waitress was holding. She walked away almost as fast as she'd come, and Dante picked up the two glasses, one in each hand.

"Your card?"

"I'm starting a tab."

"You got it like that?"

"I have to keep my woman happy."

"I'm really not that much of a drinker."

"That's okay. It works for soda, too. Drink up." He clinked his glass to hers and then turned it up, downing the contents in one swig.

Rumer held her glass in between two fingers, hesitating. She smelled hers first, then touched it gently to her lips.

"Are you going to drink it, or play with it?" Dante asked.

"What? I have to check it out first."

Dante laughed. "It's a shot. You drink it fast. You're not supposed to check it out or even taste it."

"I'm new to this."

"I can tell. Just turn it up like I did."

"You're clearly more experienced at this than I am."

"I suppose I am. But let me show you the way." Dante gazed

at her, and raised his hand without looking away. Two more shots appeared on the table. "I'll do this one with you. C'mon." He raised his glass and waited.

Rumer slowly raised hers, too, wrinkling her nose. She shrugged. What did she have to lose?

Dante counted, and on three, both of them turned their glasses up, draining them. Rumer held her breath, trying not to taste the hot liquid that was burning its way down the inside of her throat. She grimaced, then cleared her throat. "Whoa. That'll put hair on your chest."

He rubbed his hand up and down the middle of her back. "I hope not." He handed her a second shot glass.

"I don't know." Rumer's throat might never be the same. She cleared it again.

"There's nothing to know. Drink up, then dance with me, sexy."

A new warmth rushed through Rumer's body. She liked the way that sounded. As the alcohol flowed through her, it gave her a new courage. This time, she needed no help. She turned the glass up and swallowed the contents in one motion. The warmth she'd felt earlier multiplied as the smooth liquid slid down her throat.

Dante took the glass from her and put it on the table behind them, then wrapped his arms around her, kissing her on the neck.

She shivered, then giggled. They moved together and the rest of the room once again faded away. Rumer closed her eyes and leaned into Dante, her nose nestled in the bend of his neck.

"Can I cut in?" A voice dragged Rumer back to the present. She blinked as if blinded by a bright light and she pulled away from Dante. Her body felt heavy, and a sudden chill ran through her. She shivered and the room appeared to move around her.

Dante didn't let Rumer her go, and instead, spun around to face Paul. He kept his arm around her waist. Paul was standing so close, Rumer could feel the warmth of his body.

"No, I don't think you can. Get your own." Dante scowled. His voice was low, almost a growl.

"My own what?" He looked from Dante to Rumer and back again. He wasn't exactly smiling, but his face was pleasant. "Things okay over here?"

Rumer opened her mouth to speak, but Dante answered for her. "Things are fine, dude. How the hell else would they be?" He pursed his lips. "Me and Rumer were enjoying ourselves. At least we were until you interrupted us." He pulled Rumer closer, putting himself between her and Paul, and tried to get back to where they were before.

She wanted to agree with Dante, and she opened her mouth to speak again, but nothing came out. Instead, the room began to spin. "Whoa," she said, trailing off.

Paul stepped up, reaching around Dante to grab Rumer's elbow. "You sure you're okay? You don't look so good."

Rumer squinted and managed to shake her head. Her drink was way stronger than she thought it would be.

"She's fine," Dante spoke as if scolding a child. "I told you before, I can handle this without any help from you. I'll make sure she's okay." He let her go and stepped fully between her and Paul. "She's in good hands."

"I'm fine. I'm fine." Rumer's words slurred.

"You sure about that?" Paul's face darkened. "Too many times—"

Dante stepped toward Paul. "Too many times what? You didn't mind your business?"

"Guys," Rumer tried to cut in, but her words slurred,

"Just chill, Rumer," Dante said. "I've got this."

She shrank back, shocked, pressing two fingers to her temples. She wasn't sure she liked where this was going. She'd never had two people fight over her before, but it didn't look like it was going to be something she enjoyed. And what was Paul's problem? What was all the beef about?

Dante continued. "If I didn't know better, I would think you have a problem with me. Ever since I met her you've been following me around, acting like you were someone's guardian angel or something. What is your problem?"

"Let's not make a scene." Paul pushed Dante back and he almost fell into Rumer. She stumbled and both Paul and Dante lunged toward her. Dante reached her first and kept her from falling to the ground.

The tumble was enough to make Rumer snap to attention. What in the world was happening? "You know, I think I should go. I think we should go, Dante." She turned to walk away from the scene that was unfolding in front of her.

Dante grabbed her arm again, and Rumer snatched it away. His mouth dropped open. He reached out and grabbed her forearm. He snatched her toward him. "I told you, I got this. Me and Rumer are on a date."

Rumer squirmed. Dante's fingers were digging into her flesh. "You're hurting me, Dante." She pulled away, and he snatched her toward him again.

"You need to listen to me." He pulled her so hard that Rumer's feet left the ground.

"You're hurting me," Rumer said again. Her eyes were wide, and all of the people that faded away before, now seemed to be in sharp focus, and all of their eyes turned in their direction. Although the music was still playing, the room was suddenly much quieter than it had been before. All conversations and other activity in the room ceased.

"Dante." Paul's voice was heavy. "You need to check yourself." He held Dante's arm firmly.

"And you need to mind your own damned business." Dante pulled away hard. His arm snapped back and his elbow hit Rumer squarely in the mouth. She was immediately thrown backward, her hands flying up to her mouth. She was flung across the room and skidded on the floor.

The room was dead silent. Rumer's head spun and things moved in slow motion. Her stomach ached and she finally came to a stop in the middle of what would have been the dance floor. She looked up and realized that people had cleared a path and she, Paul, and Dante were in the middle of it. Rumer lay sprawled where she'd stopped, too shocked to even move. She held her breath, wishing that she would become invisible and sink through the floor.

Dante pushed Paul back with both hands. "You see what you did!" he bellowed, striding toward Rumer. "I'm so sorry. Let me help you."

Rumer tried to move and a hand reached down, pushing a napkin in her direction. She frowned. *Why would I want that?* She felt as though she were outside her body, watching everything happen. Rumer was acutely aware of all the eyes on her, all the hands that were half-covering mouths, and the people too shocked to even whisper to the person next to them.

"Dante, don't you think you've done enough? Do you want me to take you home, Rumer?" Paul's face flushed red.

Dante took the napkin, holding it to her face. "You get away from her. From us."

Rumer tried to stand, forcing him to move his hand away. Rumer's face burned with a mixture of shame and anger. How could this happen to her? She didn't know who to be more angry at. She glared at Paul, then at the people who were still staring, remembering why she hated to be the center of attention. She felt the anger draining from her, morphing into embarrassment and hurt. What had just happened? Everyone wanted a show, and this was the worst kind.

She turned to Dante, wanting to yell and cry at the same time.

Why did she have to be in the middle of their scuttle? Rumer saw the blood on the napkin in Dante's hand and any words she thought she might say caught in her throat. The room closed in on her.

What was it that was on everyone's face? Rumer's eyes finally landed on Ranisha's friends. It was then that she saw Ranisha standing in the middle of them, her arms folded across her chest. Ranisha's gaze was accusatory, and Rumer imagined all the things the girl might possibly say to her. I told you so's and smug remarks echoed in her head. They locked eyes and Rumer felt something break inside her. Everything she was holding back came through all at once and erupted in a deluge of tears.

CHAPTER NINETEEN

The mirror didn't lie. Rumor turned her head to the left and looked at the bruise on her face once more. She pulled her cheek slightly downward with her fingers. Just underneath her eye and off to the side, there it was, the evidence that last night had really happened. There was nothing that could cover it up. Rumer poked herself and flinched. The bruise on her face screamed that she had been cold-cocked right in the eye, and for the life of her, she couldn't remember how it happened. Her mouth was sore, and she remembered being hit there, but everything else was a fuzzy memory, as if it had happened to someone else.

The details were fuzzy in her brain. Paul and Dante had been talking, and then they weren't. She had been standing, and then she was bruised and laying on the floor, dying from embarrassment. And she had been cold.

It was funny how all the details were gone from her brain and there was just that one tiny thing that stood out. She remembered that the floor of the club had been cold through her clothes. She couldn't remember being hit in the face. She couldn't remember falling, but she knew those two things had happened because of the evidence on her face and the bruise on her backside. She could barely remember getting home, but she did remember that the floor had been cold. The one thing that meant nothing and everything was stuck in her brain.

Rumer touched her face again and winced. Covering this would take all of the makeup skills she'd ever acquired. Jenna knocked on the bathroom door and she jumped.

"Rumor," Jenna said. "Are you coming out soon? I have to go." Jenna's pacing made a tap dance sound outside the bathroom door.

She didn't know how she did it, but Rumer had managed to avoid Jenna seeing her face. "One second." She hadn't even really been mad about the project last night. Instead, in true Jenna form, she'd finished the work like a champ and turned it in for the both of them. By the time Rumer had come in, Jenna was in bed and there was an electronic turn-in acknowledgement in Rumer's email inbox. Jenna hadn't even questioned when Rumer told her she didn't feel well and skipped class.

"You feeling any better?" Jenna asked through the door. "Are you okay?"

"I'm good. I feel much better. Must have been something I ate." Rumer cringed as the lie slipped through her lips. It was a harmless one, or at least it was to Jenna. She finished applying her makeup and stood back to look at her handiwork. She'd become an expert in covering up overnight. *You-Tube is a wonderful thing.* "Just one more second." She tossed all of her makeup back into the bag, then turned off the light and opened the bathroom door.

Jenna leaned on the wall across from the door. "You sure

you're good?"

Rumer nodded. "Yup. Feel much better now."

Jenna stepped inside the bathroom, closing the door behind her. "I bet," she said through the door. "What did you eat?"

"No clue. We ate dinner at my mother's and then we went to a club. I nibbled on a few things there. Appetizers."

"Did you? A few things, huh?" Jenna folded her arms across her chest. "A few things like what? Wait, let me guess? Your boyfriend's *fist?*"

Rumer stopped in her tracks and turned around and glared at the door as if it were a window. "What are you talking about?"

Jenna opened the bathroom door and sat on her bed. "Don't play me, Rumer." She grabbed her pillow, holding it on her lap. "You can either tell me what happened, or leave me to believe all the gossip."

"Gossip?" Rumer bit her lip. "Are people talking about what happened *already?*"

"Really? We're going down that road? Your escapade was all over Snap Chat."

"Oh God." Rumer buried her face in her hands. "I bet it looked really bad."

"You bet? I saw a clip that looked like you'd grown superpowers and were flying through the air. Backward." Jenna put her pillow down and stood, crossing her arms across her body, more confident this time. "So, are you ready to tell me or what? I hope you're done with Dante now. That was a mess."

"Why would I be done?" It wasn't his fault. "I was the one who got between him and Paul. Whatever happened, it was between those two. I knew there was some weirdness there from the beginning."

Jenna jumped to her feet. "You're kidding me, right? Between *them*? I suppose that bruise that you were trying to cover up is what? Collateral damage?"

"It's not so bad." She paused, biting her lip. Did she really believe that? "I was in the wrong place at the wrong time, that's all. If anything, Paul is the one to blame. He started it. He was holding Dante back. He—"

"I don't know who you are." Jenna glared at her friend. "Not to mention, we were supposed to work on our project together. You blew me off. Again. Just left me out there to figure it out."

"I knew you could. Plus, it couldn't be helped. Things got out of control so fast. And it's not like I was driving myself. Dante—"

Jenna pointed, using her finger like a dagger. "Doesn't respect you enough. If he did, he would have made sure to bring you back here in time like you asked. And I'm not going to mention the physical stuff. That's just stupid and crazy. I thought you were smarter than this."

"Smarter than what? I think you're making too much of nothing. It was an accident. I was just in the wrong place at the wrong time."

"Tripping and falling, that's an accident. Being accidentally punched after we saw the man's last girlfriend with a black and blue face? That's suspect! You know it, too, or you wouldn't have tried to hide it from me last night."

Rumer opened her mouth, then closed it. "Did you call me stupid?" Tears stung her eyes and she grabbed a tissue, dabbing at her face. If she cried now, all of her cover-up handiwork would be for nothing. She inhaled as if taking in the world, but could no longer meet Jenna's stare. She didn't understand. Or she was jealous. "I don't have to explain to you."

"No, you don't." Jenna glared at Rumer. "The only person you have to answer to is yourself. I just hope you don't get hurt in the interim. Or should I say hurt again?" She headed for the door. "And you better believe the next time you leave me out there with an assignment, I'm not saving you. Trust me on that." Jenna opened the door to leave, but her way was blocked. "The only reason I did it this time was because I didn't want to have to deal with your boyfriend. But I'm sure he has a boss somewhere."

Rumer gasped. "What!" She couldn't believe what she was hearing. Jenna was supposed to be her friend, and although they weren't breaking any laws, Rumer was sure there would be some problems for Dante if Jenna caused a scene. *She wouldn't really do that, would she?*

"There's something here for you." A large floral arrangement was sitting in the middle of the doorway. "It's a damned fire hazard." Jenna stepped over the flowers, leaving them rocking back and forth, not bothering to close the door behind her. She didn't look back as she stormed down the hallway toward the steps.

Rumer didn't have time to feel sorry for herself or run after Jenna. What good would that do? It wasn't as if she could make her

169

suddenly understand what she felt or believe that Dante was not a bad person. Jenna had absolutely nothing to base her dislike on, anyway.

She picked up the flowers and used her foot to close the door to their room. Her lips curled into a smile. She temporarily pushed last night and her tiff with her friend to the back of her mind. She'd never received flowers from anyone before. She felt like she was in a romance novel. The bouquet was huge, filled with a ton of yellow daisies. It wasn't fancy, but it was certainly beautiful. Jenna was her friend, but if the shoe were on the other foot, she might be a little jealous, too.

Rumer plucked the card from the middle of the bouquet and ripped open the envelope. She already knew they would be from Dante, but hadn't expected him to send them.

I'm embarrassed and sorry. Sorry and embarrassed. I hope you will let me make things up to you.

-Dante

Rumer tapped the card on her fist, not sure how she felt. She loved the flowers, but what if Jenna was right? What if Dante really didn't care about her and what if it was not a coincidence that women around Dante got, well, hurt? She shook her head, trying to dismiss the idea. Dante was a nice guy, a gentleman, and what happened at the hotel was nothing more than a fluke, a crazy coincidence. A twinge of pain hit her and she winced at the pain in her face.

Rumer had been in a constant state of confusion since the day she'd met Dante. *How would he make it up to her?* she wondered. How would he make up for the humiliation she felt when she realized that everyone in the room was staring at her, laying in the middle of the floor? She couldn't imagine what could take that feeling away, but flowers were certainly a good start.

CHAPTER TWENTY

Paul was the last person Rumer wanted to see, yet here he was, leaning on the wall in the lobby of the Robotics building, blocking the hallway and looking as if he was waiting for her to come by. Rumer nodded, hoping that would be enough for him to let her slide by. Anger bubbled up inside her and her jaw clenched. As far as she knew, he had no business in the building at all. In fact, no more business than he'd had to be in the lab like he'd been the other day.

"Rumer." He sang her name as if they were old friends. She glared at him, her face hard. It was his fault that she'd been embarrassed, no, mortified. It was his fault that her face was all bruised. "I know you don't want to talk to me."

"You're right, I don't."

"Wow." The smile that had been on his face disappeared. "I just wanted to catch up to you before class. To apologize."

Rumer crossed her arms. "Go ahead."

"You don't have to be so salty."

Rumer couldn't believe he even had the audacity to even talk to her. "No? I suppose I should feel good about the bruises on my face? About the way everyone stares at me now. If you'd just minded your own business, none of this would have happened."

"Is that what you think? That this is somehow my fault? Oh, no, sister, trust me when I tell you that you would have ended up hurt one way or the other. Dante is a bit of a hot head, you have no idea. I—"

"You have no idea what you're talking about." Rumer's voice had grown steadily louder.

"I don't? I've known him a long time. Did you think you were the first?"

Rumer's face flushed with anger. "You're making a scene." She crossed her arms in front of her.

Paul looked around. "If people are staring at you, it's your own fault for yelling like you don't have good sense."

Looking injured, Rumer's eyes darted around the hallway. She took a deep breath, blinking back tears. "I'm sorry," she said. "Can we start over?" She felt even more overwhelmed than she had when she first looked in the mirror this morning. Why did it seem as if things were spiraling out of control? Last week this time, she'd felt like she had everything under control. At this point, she was no longer sure of anything.

"Fine with me." He paused, his face tense, then sighed. "I apologize for interrupting your date. Sorry for what happened to you. No one deserves that."

She nodded. "Apology accepted." Maybe if they acted civilly, it would be as if nothing had happened, right? Rumer knew that made no sense as she was thinking it. How many times before had pretending something wasn't happening fixed anything? She held her chin higher.

Paul stepped closer, lowering his voice. "Look, Jenna is worried about you, and frankly, I think I am, too. You can come to me if you need to."

"What? Come to you for what? And just why would I do that?" Rumer's head spun. "You and Jenna are a team now? You both need to mind your own damned business."

"Well, hello Paul. Rumer. What did I miss?" Dante came around the corner and stopped, his eyes darting from Rumer to Paul.

Paul stepped back and away from Rumer. He cleared his throat. "What's up, man?"

Rumer looked away like a child scolded for misbehavior.

Dante's mouth was drawn into a thin line. "Rumer, I expect to see you in the lab after class. We have to make up for the time you missed yesterday." He was using his indifferent and professional voice again.

Confusion flooded over her. "Sure. No problem." She got it. Rumer was beginning to see how this worked, but professional Dante still had a hint of anger in his words, making this almost silent treatment sting even more. Other than the few words he'd said, Rumer felt dismissed.

Dante glared at Paul, pausing for what seemed like an eternity. "Good, then. Paul? Can we walk and talk?"

Paul nodded and they strode off together, leaving Rumer to watch them go.

CHAPTER TWENTY-ONE

Her pride was more hurt than she'd imagined, but she still accepted Dante's offer of a do-over, and so far, so good. Dinner had been wonderful. Rumer had enjoyed eating things she couldn't even pronounce.

"I almost feel guilty." She blushed.

"For?" Dante smiled, looking deep into her eyes. His dimples flashed and Rumer felt her heartbeat skip. She pressed her knees together, unused to the stirring she was feeling throughout her body.

"For spending all your money. This was expensive."

"It was. But don't you think you're worth it?" He rubbed the back of her hand. "As beautiful as you are, someone should be spending everything they have to get your attention. Don't worry about it."

Was she worth it? It didn't feel quite right, not to mention that she had to endure numerous bouts of eye-rolling and mean mugging from Jenna. Things still weren't right between them. "I know how it is. I'm a student, too."

"It's okay. I get paid for teaching, and I have a stipend as a grad student. I wouldn't have brought you here if I couldn't swing it. I'll let you know if we have to wash any dishes."

"Well, thank you." Rumer looked down at her hands. She

didn't know what else to say about it. "Jenna said—"

Dante's face darkened. "I'm not interested in what Jenna had to say right now. I'm focused on making things right between us. I need you to be able to see the real me." He paused. "I'm sure our friends will have a whole lot to say, but we're both grown. We can make our own decisions. And I've decided to spoil you."

Rumer giggled. She had yet to think of herself as being grown. Despite the clothes and makeup and even living in the dorms, she felt like a little girl most days. She still felt as if she had to ask permission, like she wasn't the one that had the final say in almost anything that went on in her life.

"Let me make you happy, Rumer. I feel like we have a special kinship, and I don't want one bad night to mess it up." He extended his hand across the table to her.

Rumer paused. She wanted to be with Dante. It was exciting to have someone like him interested in her. He was like a knight in shining armor that had walked out of a fairy tale or something. "It didn't mess it up." Rumer didn't care what people thought this time. She knew that if she put him off too long, there would be someone else, like Ranisha, waiting to take her place. She took his hand.

"Do you feel what I feel?"

Rumer nodded. She felt something, but he wasn't sure what. When you broke it down, she was feeling a lot of things, and most of them were good.

"I know what you need, Rumer."

"You do?"

"Of course I do. We're connected in a way that I have never been with anyone else. After this class is over, I want us to be together for real."

Rumer's heart pounded in her chest. No one had ever said those words to her before. Jenna would say it was all a con, but she refused to believe that. Dante was pouring his heart out to her in the restaurant in a way that could only be real. It was almost too much to understand. She had become grown up and sexy and popular, all in the space of a week. College was the best thing that had ever happened to her. She didn't know how to answer him.

He pulled out his phone. "I'm sorry, I have to answer this one. Do you mind?" The soft smile on his face made Rumer melt.

"No, it's fine. I understand completely." He probably had a lot going on with his teaching assistantship.

Dante sent a text, then put his phone back on the seat next to him. "So, what do you say to us getting out of here? We can go back to my place and just chill. Away from everyone. We'll stop on the way at a spot I know, first. Drop in and listen to some music. A friend of mine is in a band I think you will enjoy."

Rumer smiled. "Sounds good." No one had ever wanted to take her anywhere before other than maybe Macdonald's, and Dante had managed to take her on several dates in a row. And now live music? She'd only been to a concert once in her life. Rumer felt like she was going to enjoy being grown.

After three glasses of wine, Rumer's head swam. She should have followed her gut and turned them down, but after the first one, she'd felt so at ease that she couldn't. The music had been good, and Dante felt so amazing next to her that nothing could seem wrong.

She pulled her sweater tighter around her as she waited for him to get his door open. He ran his hand down the middle of her back, right between her shoulder blades and she shivered.

"Sorry. My key is a little bent. We'll be inside in a minute." He removed the key and put it back in again. In reality, he was stalling. His roomie hadn't answered his text, but he wanted to give him a few extra minutes to straighten up the place. They weren't messy, but they weren't exactly neat, either, at least not woman neat.

Finally, the door opened. He stepped aside to let Rumer go first, holding his breath. He glanced past and gave the room a once over. Things were straight. Tyrone wouldn't let him down. He inhaled. He'd even remembered to spray air freshener and crack a window.

"It's chilly. You guys don't believe in heat?"

"My apologies. You have a seat." He strode across the room and shut the window, then turned the thermostat up a few degrees. "I'll get you a drink. You'll be warm in no time."

Rumer let herself sink into the leather sofa, enjoying its plushness. Dante's apartment was much nicer than she imagined it would be. What kind of student got to live like this? "You have a roommate?" She ran her fingers over a throw pillow. *How many men had throw pillows?* His student reality was obviously different than hers,

180

Rumer thought

He answered from the small kitchen, just a few feet away. "I do. Two actually. You know Paul. He's not here. And the other's probably in his room. Asleep. It's his favorite pastime."

"Oh, we won't be disturbing him, will we?"

"Doubtful. There isn't much that can wake him. He practically sleeps like he's dead." He handed her a small tumbler of liquid. "Here."

"What's this?"

"A gut warmer. It'll knock the chill right out of you. Can't have my baby being cold."

Rumer melted. Did he just say *my baby*? Did they officially have a thing?

Dante kissed Rumer, fast and hard. He pressed his mouth to hers, holding her in the small of her back, pulling her to him.

Her mouth opened in surprise and her hands immediately went to his shoulders in an attempt to push him away. He kissed her harder, and she melted, giving in to the steady motion of his kiss. Her heartbeat thundered in her ears. His lips felt more amazing than she imagined they could.

Rumer inhaled, taking in the scent of the cold, crisp air that still flooded the room. With her eyes closed, the effects of the alcohol deepened. The space inside her head swirled in darkness. Dante made her feel so special, everything was jumbled. Or maybe it was the alcohol. Or something else. At that moment, Rumer didn't know and didn't care.

Suddenly frightened, Rumer was confused. What was she doing? How did she even get here? They were grooving to the music of his friend's band, and then they left the club. Dante's hands had been everywhere, all over her, all at the same time. Her body was electrified.

Sensing her hesitation, Dante pulled away. "You okay?" he asked. "Doesn't it feel good? Let me make you feel good."

It did feel good. "I guess so." But that didn't make it necessarily feel right. Rumer pulled back.

"You guess? C'mon, girl. Relax. Don't you trust me?"

Rumer nodded. At least she thought she trusted him. How could she not? Dante was attractive, smart, accomplished and popular. And he was interested in her. Who didn't want that?

"I want to make you feel good," he said, pulling her toward him again. "Don't you want that?"

She did, but she didn't. Rumer pulled away again. "Wait,"

Dante sat back. "C'mon. There is no need for games." He put his hand on her knee, caressing it gently. "I knew we were on the same page when you agreed to come." He smiled and moved his hand slowly up her leg, his fingers flirting with the edge of her skirt.

Rumer gasped. Her whole body tingled. Dante leaned in to kiss her one more time, and Rumer was once again flooded with doubt. "I'm sorry, Dante." She shook her head, "I think I should go."

Instead of stopping, Dante pushed his hand further up her skirt. "Please, girl. You know you want this. I promise I'll be good to you. You'll be begging me for more." He ran his fingers along the lace of her panties.

Rumer slammed her hand down over his, pushing his hand back. "Stop it, for real, Dante. I want to go." Without thinking, Rumer slapped Dante across the face.

"What the fuck?" he yelled. "Oh no, you didn't. I don't know what you think this is."

Dante stood up and grabbed Rumer by the throat, lifting her off the sofa. She grabbed his forearm with both hands and tried to pull his hand away, struggling against his grasp. He swung her around in one motion, carrying her across the room, pinning her face to the apartment wall.

Rumer saw stars. White lights floated in front of her face like in a cartoon. Time slowed down as her face was pushed up against the wall. If cartoons were correct, if nothing changed, she knew what would come next. She would lose consciousness and pass out. Her stomach felt sick.

Dante pressed himself behind her, reaching around and up her dress. He kissed her neck, her collar. He breathed in her ear, all the while holding her in place.

Rumer's heart pounded in her head and tears ran down her face. "Please," she said, pleading with Dante to stop. She willed herself to stop fighting him. If she did that, maybe he would stop, too. The neurons in her brain fired as she struggled to remember what she was supposed to do in this situation. What had they said to do to when you want someone to stop, and why wasn't Dante listening to what she was saying?

"I knew you wanted me," Dante rasped in her ear. "No one pushes me away."

She stopped struggling, no longer able to hear or feel anything.

"That's what I thought." Dante's eyes were pinpoints. "I'm going to give you what you came here for."

CHAPTER TWENTY-TWO

The locker room was teeming with people. No one looked up as Dante entered. He preferred it like this. People were coming back to campus for the fall semester already, and more people meant no one would question his actions, leaving him to blend into campus better.

As he worked his way back to the corner of the locker room where he kept his stuff, Dante enjoyed the added liveliness. There was a buzz in the air of male laughter. He nodded at a few people as he passed, giving them the heads up that was exchanged only by men of color.

Tyrone and Paul were in their usual locker row, both wrapped in towels from the waist down. Tyrone danced, mimicking some dance he'd seen in a video, snapping his fingers in time to the music that played on the small speaker attached to his iPod.

"You're supposed to be educated," Paul sneered. "Can you turn that down? Other people might not want to hear all that."

Dante dropped his bag onto the locker-room bench and removed his shirt. "Don't tell me that Mr. Social Consciousness major has a problem with Rap Genius now? Leave a brother alone with his music if that is what he likes."

"Wow. Just wow." Paul leaned back on his locker. "But I guess

I shouldn't be surprised."

Dante stopped what he was doing. "What's that supposed to mean? You don't like rap? You gonna shoot me now because my music is too loud?"

"I like music, period. But I like lyrics that *say* something."

Tyrone stepped into his underwear. "These say something. You can't tell me that this is not your jam! Lil Wayne, man!"

"I know who it is," Paul said. "I suppose you like Chief Keef, too. All of these rappers are misogynistic idiots."

Dante laughed. "Please. More like clever wordsmiths. And don't act like it's just rappers that have lyrics like that. Chis Brown ain't a rapper. He had some like that, too. Country music does it."

Paul held up his hand. "I can't get into this now with you two. Just turn the music down so other people aren't disturbed, a'ight?"

Tyrone made a face at Dante, but turned the music down some. "Yeah, we don't want to get kicked out of the men's locker room for having fun, do we?"

Paul scowled, but Dante and Tyrone both burst into laughter. Dante opened his locker and took out his pink pen. He made a hash mark next to the last one he'd drawn there.

"Nah, man! Say it isn't so." Tyrone looked at Dante with amazement. "You get more action than James Bond. Don't tell me you cracked that young hottie. I can't believe she even let you in after the other night. What's the secret?"

"No secret. Just Mack Daddy."

Tyrone gave Dante a high-five. "Did you use that stuff?"

Dante held his finger to his lips, signaled to Tyrone to keep it down. "I can't reveal my secrets." His voice was barely above a whisper.

Paul spun around, his eyes narrow. "You need to check yourself before someone gets hurt messing with that shit."

"No one is getting hurt. They're getting—"

"Do you hate women? Wasn't your mother a woman?" Paul's chest heaved. He walked toward Dante, his fists clenching.

Dante held up his hands in mock surrender. "What the hell, man? Why are your panties all in a bunch? This ain't anything new, and how I bed my women has nothing to do with you. It's what I do. I smash the hotties."

"She's not even a freshman. If you hurt her, I—"

"You'll what, Paul? Beat my ass?" Dante paused, running his hand over the top of his head and licking his lips. "What's your story, man? This is the natural order of things. It's the birds and the bees. We sing about it. We talk about it. Dog chases cat. Chill."

"Don't you tell me to chill. That girl is someone's child. Because of dudes like you, my sister had to drop out of school."

"I'm not some dude, and unless there's something you didn't tell me, she is not your sister."

Paul slammed his locker. "You know what? I hope you have a daughter one day. I just hope karma doesn't come to bite you in the ass when you do."

Dante didn't answer Paul. He and Tyrone looked on but said nothing as Paul stormed away. He'd get over it. He always did.

CHAPTER TWENTY-THREE

The throbbing in Rumer's head was so loud she couldn't really hear anything else. She'd thought a shower would make it better, and had taken two, but nothing had changed. If anything, she felt worse than she had when she woke up. The shower hadn't helped the feeling that her skin was crawling, either. She felt like she'd just worked out hard and hadn't showered in weeks, as if she were both exhausted *and* unclean.

Advil was her friend. She searched through the lint in the bottom of her backpack for the few pills she knew to be hiding there. They were so old that the color had started to wear off of them, but she didn't care, swallowing them without water.

Every other breath left her queasy and her eyes stung, but she couldn't skip class. It didn't matter how friendly she was with the instructor, she couldn't afford to not do well. Her mother would be so disappointed if she did. *She'd be disappointed anyway.* The voice in her head was loud and clear.

Rumer didn't want to move too fast for fear that she might sweat. She'd read somewhere that alcohol molecules hurt when they came through your pores, and it was bad enough she was fighting the need to vomit. She couldn't take much more. Her mother's voice rang in her head. "You got to pay when you play." *Momma was right,* she thought. She was certainly paying now, for everything.

Jenna had already gone, leaving her to feign sleep in the bed. Rumer was thankful for small miracles. She searched her mind, trying to piece together last night's events. She didn't remember much between the third glass of wine and the time she unlocked her door to her dorm. She couldn't even remember if Dante had driven her home or if she'd taken an Uber.

He'd kissed her and she kissed him back and it felt good. She also remembered that she wanted to stop. And that was where her memory ended. Her body had a new soreness to it that was unfamiliar. She hurt on her legs and her collarbone and places she didn't even want to think about. Her lip was also busted. She'd discovered quite a few bruises in the shower. Thankfully, clothes would cover them up.

When she got to the lobby, Jenna was there, in the coffee line, but she looked away as soon as Rumer made eye contact. She couldn't still be mad from the other day, could she? Rumer hopped into the line, a few people behind Jenna. Coffee would help. It helped everything feel better. Hopefully it would take away the feeling that she'd been hit by a truck, too.

Rumer sipped her coffee while walking, with Jenna just a few steps ahead of her. Jenna had taken off immediately after she got her drink and made no efforts to talk to Rumer, so she slowed down, too. It didn't make sense to take the chance that Jenna might ask questions she didn't want to answer.

By the time she made it to the classroom, Jenna was engaged in conversation with someone else, facing the opposite direction. A twinge of guilt hit Rumer. She felt just a little bad about not sharing with her friend, but she wasn't in the sharing mood. Instead, she wanted to crawl back into her bed and hibernate. She did miss the gentle ribbing about how late she'd stayed out and what she had done that they might have shared a few weeks ago.

Jenna would know what she should do. Rumer wanted to tell her friend everything about Saturday, about the wine, the other drinks, even about Dante, at least what she could remember, but she didn't want Jenna to do that judgy thing she sometimes did or force her to ask herself hard questions.

The students were talking and looking at their phones when they entered. Dante was late. Rumer frowned. He was late for the first time that semester. A part of her was relieved and she realized that she was actually holding her breath, wishing that Dante didn't show up at all. She didn't want to face him.

Rumer found a seat and opened her book. She didn't want to make small talk with anyone. After a few minutes, someone entered and the hush reserved for the instructor came over the room as everyone stopped what they were doing and looked up. It wasn't him, but Rumer noticed several girls staring in her direction. One held a phone, and Jenna was in the middle of the group. She smiled, and they looked away, Jenna included.

They got quiet and moved to their seats, but no one said anything or returned her smile. Jenna wouldn't even look at her.

A feeling of dread crept into the pit of Rumer's stomach. What now? she wondered? What had happened that they knew about or that she couldn't remember?

By the time Dante arrived, Rumer was full-on in the depths of worry, feeling sick to her stomach for reasons she didn't understand. A few beads of sweat appeared on her forehead. She looked up and her heartrate skyrocketed. The familiar, warm, fuzzy feeling she'd had when she saw Dante had been replaced. She felt even more sweaty and hot and she couldn't breathe.

Dante didn't look her way, instead it felt as if he did everything in his power to look around her. Rumer sat at the desk with her palms down. She pressed so hard against the beige melamine surface that her fingers began to lose color.

Finally, she was unable to take it anymore. There was no way that Rumer could sit in the classroom. There was no point. The pounding in her head made it impossible to hear anything that Dante had said. She glanced at the clock. There were only a few minutes to go, but if she didn't leave now, things could get bad.

She didn't even take her things. Rumer grabbed her phone and bolted from the classroom, making a beeline for the nearest restroom. She bumped into a girl on the way, and was vaguely aware of books hitting the floor, but she couldn't stop. Rumer barely made it to a bathroom stall before she felt herself retching. She emptied what felt like everything she'd eaten for a week into the commode.

Finally, so empty that it felt like the sides of her stomach were rubbing together, Rumer stopped vomiting. She felt hot all over, and her face was covered with sweat. She checked her ponytail, hoping that there were no remnants of her escapades caught in her hair. She tore off some toilet paper and dabbed at her face.

The bathroom mirror told her the story she already knew. She looked a mess. Her face was ashen, and her eyes were surrounded by dark circles that were beginning to show through her makeup. She wanted to wash her face, imagining the relief that cool water would bring, but dreaded the thought of removing the makeup that she'd worked so hard to put on. There was no way she was going to walk around the campus with bruises showing. She'd have to hide in the lab the rest of the day as it was.

Her class would be over in three minutes, and Rumer planned to wait outside the room until everyone left to get her things. Jenna might not be talking to her, but her sudden departure from the classroom might change her mind. Rumer didn't want to chance that, so she took the long way back to the classroom. She kept her head down as she walked. There was no chance she would enjoy running into anyone that might have been at the hotel. Her skin crawled every time a pair of eyes hit her. She felt as if everyone was staring through her.

Rumer was almost home free. She felt herself relax just a little. She was so busy looking behind her as she turned the corner to the classroom that she walked right into Ranisha. "Excuse me," she said. It took a moment for the person in front of her to register.

Ranisha leaned back on the wall. "You look a mess. How are things working out with Dante?" she sneered at Rumer. "I tried to tell you."

Just then, even the air felt heavy. Rumer couldn't control herself. She burst into tears. Ranisha's mouth dropped open and she paused for a second. Her eyes darkened and she grabbed Rumer's arm, pulling her into the nearest room.

"Get yourself together." Ranisha's voice was filled with a mixture of disdain and pity. " Dante is a very passionate person. If you're going to deal with him, you have to be able to take what comes with it. This is the price."

"The price?" She sniffled, wiping her face with the back of her hand.

Ranisha sighed heavily. "All that fineness wrapped up in one person. Did you think this was a fairy tale? Let me guess? You put your little freak 'em dress on, he got your drunk, and you can't remember the rest?"

How did she know? Rumer's tears stopped.

"Uh, huh. Just as I thought." She gave Rumer a once over. "You should know better. I bet you looked good. I bet you gladly led him on."

"No, I didn't." Rumer had a flash of her mother. She didn't like the way this sounded at all. "I said no. I didn't want—"

"Girl, it doesn't matter what we want. They take it, no matter what. You had to want something, or you wouldn't have been, wait, where? At his house? A hotel?"

Rumer's tears started flowing again.

"He made all of your drinks, didn't he? Things never change. Did you see him do it?"

Rumer shook her head and fought back more tears. She couldn't remember when he'd made drinks.

"What did you think would happen? I saw you out with him. You looked real cute with your midriff showing." She shook her head. "He's just a man. You can't blame him. That is the way they are." She paced the room. "If you can't take it, just go away. Crawl back to your little high school and let the grown-ups play grown-up games. Me and Dante have history, and you're messing with that. If you're not willing to do what it takes to treat him right, just go away so someone who knows what to do can take over."

"Are you serious? Why would anyone—"

"I am very serious. I do what is necessary to keep my man."

"What?"

"You heard me." She stepped closer to Rumer. "You ain't ready for this yet. Let me guess? You want to tell someone? Honey, ain't no one listening. Trust me."

"You don't know—"

"I do know. One question? Did he say you were special? Did you think you were?"

Rumer opened her mouth, and closed it again. She wrapped her arms cross her stomach to try and ward off the nagging pain she had there.

"We are all the same to him, or didn't you know that?" Ranisha reached into her bag. "Here's a tissue. Go home and play with your dolls." She tossed it at Rumer, who caught it in mid-air.

She watched, stunned, as Ranisha stormed from the room.

Unsure of whether Ranisha was trying to scare or comfort her, Rumer wiped her face and took a deep breath. Her day just got worse.

CHAPTER TWENTY-FOUR

"Can we talk about that girl?" Ranisha's voice bellowed throughout the Robotics lab. "Dante! I know you're in here somewhere." She pushed a stool out of her way as she made a beeline for the back of the lab, to the area where the graduate students had small working offices.

Dante met her half way. "Ranisha," he said. "Why are you here? You might not have anything to do, but I have lots." He scrolled through his phone, not bothering to make eye contact. "You're going to have to keep your voice down. I'm working here."

"You got a minute?"

"Not really. I've got papers to grade. I'm very busy."

"No time for me, now? That's how you want to play it?" Ranisha's voice got progressively louder. "I can say what I have to say right here if you want everyone in earshot to know your business." She looked around the room, talking loudly for effect. Her face burned with anger now. "You can act all brand new if you want to, but I will call you out right here and I don't care who hears what I have to say. Maybe if I scream it, then people will listen."

A frustrated look came over Dante and he shifted his weight from foot to foot. "Okay," he said finally. He grabbed Ranisha's arm.

She tried to pull away. "You can let me go."

"I could, but I'm not going to." He half dragged and half-pushed Ranisha toward his office. "You wanted me. You got me." He led her back to a small windowed room.

"You're hurting me." She tried to pull away, but Dante held onto her harder.

"Am I? Isn't this what you wanted? You usually like it rough." He pushed her through the small door and closed it behind them. A few people in the main lab looked around. Dante glared at them, as if challenging them with his eyes. They all eventually went back to what they were doing.

Dante shoved Ranisha down into a chair. She immediately stood up. "I want to stand up."

He shoved her back down again. "No one cares what you want, or don't you get that?"

Her backside made contact with the wooden chair so hard, she felt it all the way through to her teeth. Ranisha cringed as tears sprang to her eyes.

"You're going to cry now? What happened to big, bad 'I'm going to shout it from the rooftops?' What do you want, Ranisha?"

She took a deep breath, then swallowed hard. This was not how she intended things to go. "I want to know what the deal is." She rubber her arm.

"What deal?"

"Oh, you're stupid now? The deal between us. You keep putting me off. I was under the impression—"

"That's you're problem right there."

"What?"

"You assumed some shit, didn't you? I made you no promises."

Ranisha reeled back as if slapped. "What?" she said, again. "We dated."

"We hung out. It's not the same thing. Just because I bought you dinner a couple of times don't mean we are getting married."

"That's not what I meant. I didn't think that."

"You sure, Ranisha? You think I don't know you've been mean-mugging Rumer?" He leaned back on his desk.

"Is she your girlfriend now?" Her eyes pleaded with him. "But we made love. You said that you would take care of me."

Dante laughed. "Did I? I meant sexually not for life."

Tears streamed from Ranisha's eyes. She wrapped her arms around her body. "I thought—"

He held up his hand to stop her. "You shouldn't have. You women think that just because we do the deed, we're bonded for life. It's a biological function." He ran his head over his head, letting out a sigh. "Look, I like you. You're nice. But you're not smart. I mean, I do thank you for sharing some time with me. We had fun, but a booty call is a booty call. Let's not try to make it more."

Anger bubbled up through Ranisha's tears. She stood up and lunged toward him. "You are a horrible person. It wasn't that good anyway. I only did it because you made me feel like I had no choice. I could go and report you." Her voice was shrill.

"You'd better back up off me, woman!" Dante's voice rattled the office window. "Report me for what? You're a joke."

"You drugged me."

He leaned in close, leaving his nose almost touching hers. "Did I? You wanted to be with me. Everyone saw us out beforehand. I told you that you weren't smart. Who are they going to believe? You, a barely passing student with a colorful past? Or me? An athlete? Better than a 4.0 GPA? Church-going. Respected. Upstanding. I dare you to try."

Ranisha's body was wracked with sobs now, her shoulders heaving. She covered her face with her hands. Dante was right. No one would believe anything she said.

"I'm going to need you to get yourself together. I've gotta get my papers graded, and I know you have something you have to do, too." He turned his back to her, leaving her sobbing on the chair and answered his phone. "Let yourself out, Ranisha. I'll catch you later."

CHAPTER TWENTY-FIVE

Rumer's body felt like lead. After being ignored by her best friend, throwing up everything she'd ever eaten, then having to deal with Ranisha, all Rumer wanted to do was crawl in between her covers and sleep for a week. Her hand opened the door to the dorm room easily, and her heart sank. A few tears sprang to her eyes. Jenna had beat her back to the room and the last thing Rumer wanted was to fight right now. She had nothing left.

She took in a deep breath and entered her room. Just as she'd thought, Jenna was sitting right inside the door. They locked eyes and Rumer felt naked under her friend's piercing gaze.

"I just don't have time, Jenna." Rumer dragged herself to her bed. "I need a nap."

Jenna intercepted her, and instead of talking or asking the questions Rumer thought she would, she wrapped her arms around Rumer and hugged.

Rumer had no idea what to do. She stood there, frozen and awkward. "Okay."

"You should have told me." Jenna hugged her for so long it felt awkward.. "Told you what?"

"Did he hit you?"

"What are you talking about?" Rumer said, but she knew exactly what her friend was talking about. Shame crept over her. They sat on opposite beds.

"It was all over Tumblr. Someone posted that Dante likes to be rough. They said that you two were at the set together and he practically dragged you out by your hair. You're a meme."

Rumer sighed and fell back on her bed, covering her face with a pillow. "Of course, if it's on the Internet, it must be true." She didn't want Jenna to see her face. "Dante is a nice guy. He didn't drag me anywhere. I went willingly."

Jenna frowned. "Really? Shall I show you?" She took out her phone, holding it up for Rumer to see.

She tried to avert her eyes. "You thought wrong. We left there and went to his place. I wanted to."

"Hmmm. Okay. Everyone is talking about it." She paused. "So, are you going to tell me?"

Rumer wanted to tell her, but she couldn't. Although she still didn't remember everything, the aches and pains in her body were telling her more than she wanted to know. She burst into tears. She pulled her pillow back onto her face.

"Um, okay. I don't need to know that bad."

Rumer cried even harder.

Jenna came over and sat on her friend's bed. "I've never seen you like this," she said, rubbing Rumer on her back. "You can tell me anything. I'm sorry for earlier. I was just so angry with you for acting, you know, not like yourself."

"I'm sorry, too." It was too heavy. Rumer had to tell someone. "I hate him. He just seemed so nice." Her lips quivered and her body quaked as the memory of the night before came rushing back. Before she knew what was happening, she'd told the whole story.

Jenna listened quietly, rubbing her on the back the entire time. Anger flashed across her face.

"Ranisha said I deserved what I got." The words tumbled form her lips. "She said I stole her man and wore skimpy clothes and—"

"Shhh. That's nonsense. I don't know why people say things like that. How could you deserve to be treated badly based on the way you are dressed? Or where you stand? Blaming the victim is bullshit." She held her friend, and her insides bled for her as she listened. They both knew that one thing Ranisha said was half-right. No one would want to hear Rumer's story, and no one would believe what she said. Half of the people that knew about it would say that she'd asked for whatever happened to her, wanted it even.

"It's the same old story every time this happens. I don't understand why people want to blame the victim."

"It's my word against his." Rumer sobbed now.

There was nothing to say, and they both knew it. If she made a fuss, only Rumer would be Hester Primm.

"Maybe," Jenna said. "We'll figure something out. People like Dante always get theirs one way or the other."

Rumer let her friend hug her again, and hoped that she was right. "I don't know why I didn't listen. You tried to warn me. Ranisha tried to warn me—"

"You can't count her. She has her own agenda. A really strange one. No one ever listens to the ex-girlfriend."

"That's true. But I think Paul tried to warn me, too. And he's Dante's friend."

Jenna nodded. "I don't know what his deal is, but I think we should find out."

"What are you talking about? I think I've had my fill of Dante and his friends. I just want things to go back to the way they were."

"I feel you, but I think we should talk to Paul and see if he can help us."

"Help us how? We can't *undo* anything. No one will listen to what I have to say. Stuff like this has been in the news at campuses all over the country." She paused. "I hate that I am a statistic. What happens if I report him? He fails me! I can't afford to fail this class. That will look terrible on my transcript. I really messed this up. Didn't I?"

Jenna rubbed her friend's back. "I hate this, too. And no, we can't undo anything, but maybe we can help someone else."

"I feel so stupid." Tears started to flow again. "I know better, I really do. I was losing myself so quickly. I know all the warning signs. I lived with it for so many years. My parents..."

Jenna shushed her. "Just because you know doesn't mean you're immune. Even I have to admit that Dante is fine. It's so easy to get lost when someone looks like that."

"He's smooth." Half a smile peeked through Rumer's tears.

"And that. There's that. Um."

Rumer and Jenna burst into laughter, and Rumer wiped her eyes. "I guess fineness doesn't exempt you from being an asshole, either. I just want this semester to be over so I can go home and never see him again."

Jenna wanted that, too. She nodded but didn't comment. There was no way they would be able to avoid Dante and get a passing grade in their class. She had the feeling that it was going to be a long two weeks.

CHAPTER TWENTY-SIX

"Hey, Tyrone." Paul's voice was low as he greeted Tyrone in the empty locker room. "What's up?"

"Not a thing, my man." He reached his hand out to Paul for their customary bro-shake. "I didn't expect to see you here so early. And what's up with your face? Did someone die?" He stared at his friend. "You're the one that normally has on a happy face without having any coffee."

Paul shook his head. "Nothing, man. I'm just sick and tired."

Tyrone laughed. "Of what? What kind of problems could you possibly have?"

Paul took a deep breath and paused. The silence of the locker room enveloped them, highlighting the loudness of the dripping faucets back in the showers.

Paul glanced at his watch. It was early. There would be no people for at least another hour. He looked around before speaking. "Don't you ever get tired of Dante and his shit? I mean, he's been running over people all of his life."

"I don't know what you mean. I mind my business. You know he's my boy. We go way back."

"I hear you. We go way back, too. He and I have known each other since we were kids." He paused. "Have you talked to Rumer lately?"

"You mean that young thing from his class? Nah. Why would I do that? You know how Dante is once he decides that someone is on his list. That girl has been chosen. I don't want to cross Dante. Na'mean?"

"No, I don't know what you mean. Maybe that's what he needs. Someone to ask him hard questions."

Tyrone held up his hands. "I let him do him and I mind my business. It's not my place to ask those kinds of questions."

"It's not? Isn't that what friends do? Hold other friends accountable for the stuff they do? Are you afraid of him or something?"

"I'm not afraid of anyone." Tyrone sat back. "Why're you tripping?"

"I'm just asking the hard questions. You can't tell me that if that girl was your sister, you wouldn't have a problem with the way he did her."

"But she's not my sister. And she's not yours, either."

"No, I guess she's not, but she could be, right?" Paul cocked his head to the side as he waited for Tyrone to respond. "Are you even getting what I'm saying? I'm not asking you if you tried to step to her lately. Just, have you *seen* her? Talked to her like a human being?"

Tyrone sat on the end of the bench and stared at Paul. "You really are tripping. Where are you going with this? I have no reason to talk to that girl."

Paul licked his lips as if carefully choosing his next words. "I guess you're right about that. How about Ranisha? Have you talked to her?"

"Again, I say to you, why would I?" His eyes narrowed. "What's going on?"

Paul opened his locker. "I've talked to Ranisha. She's a mess. And I've talked to Jenna, Rumer's friend. Apparently Rumer barely comes out of her room." He sighed, shaking his head. "Did you see the videos?"

"You know I try to stay off social media."

"You're the only one." He paused. "I'm just tired."

"You should mind your business. You can't be hating on a brother because he spits game so well that these young ladies are all messed up in their heads. He's not committing any crimes."

"Isn't he, though? Can you say that for sure? Last I checked, drugging people wasn't legal." He raised his eyebrows.

"Keep your voice down. I ain't seen nothing. I don't know nothing."

"I see how this goes. You can't keep closing your eyes to this stuff. If he is willing to do it to them, what will he do to you?"

"Whoa, man. It ain't like that. I trust Dante."

"So did both of them."

"There's a code among men. Bro's before ho's. That's Shakespeare."

Paul frowned. "Really, Ty? This is not what Shakespeare meant. I know you're smarter than that."

Tyrone stood up, pausing to tie his shoe. "We can sit here and debate this all day, but I ain't going to. I gotta get my run on. You should do the same."

"So you're just going to change the subject, then? It's like that?"

"What it's like is I can't solve all the world's problems in a few minutes and I'm running out of time. I have things that I have to get done today. You can come with me if you think you can keep up."

"Whatever, man. I'll just keep my thoughts to myself." He stood up and turned his back to Tyrone, his brow furrowed. He shook his head and played with the lock on his locker for a bit, waiting for Tyrone to leave.

He stood there for what seemed like an eternity, wanting to be sure that he was alone. He leaned on the locker, his stomach tied in knots. Paul closed his eyes and opened them again. *There is no right answer*, he told himself. *Time's running out.* The voice in his head debated with himself, but he knew what he had to do.

CHAPTER TWENTY-SEVEN

"Rumer, you have got to get up." Jenna opened the shades in their dorm room and tried to pull the covers off of her friend.

Rumer grunted, grabbing the tops of her bedding. She drew it around herself closer, covering her head.

"You've been in this room for almost a week. There is no way you are going to pass this class if you don't show up. I can't cover for you anymore."

"I never asked you to cover for me. Go away."

"No, I won't. And if you don't get up and shower, I'm calling your mother." She wrinkled her nose. "You're making the room smell."

"Go somewhere." Rumer turned over, facing the wall.

A knock on the door interrupted Jenna's answer. Frustrated, she sighed heavily. "I would say don't move, but I doubt that will happen anyway." She stormed toward the door. "I don't know who would be knocking at eight in the morning." She flung the door open.

Jenna couldn't believe that Ranisha had the balls to actually come to their dorm room. "Hey."

"Excuse me." Instead of waiting for an invitation, Ranisha

stormed past Jenna and into their room. She walked up to Rumer's bed and ripped the covers off of her. "Get up," she demanded.

"What the hell?" Rumer sat straight up in bed, trying to cover herself with pillows.

Ranisha fumed. "Don't you want to fight?"

"I have no desire to fight you. You're crazy."

"Not me. Him." Ranisha paused, looking from Rumer to Jenna. "We can go together."

Jenna came up behind Ranisha now. "I'm listening."

Rumer sank back into the bed. "Gimme my covers. Go where together? You really are crazy."

"I'm going to ignore that." She started folding Rumer's blanket. "We can go to the administration."

"What good would that do? No one will believe us, you know that. Don't you watch television? And I can't even remember what happened, not fully."

"Of course you can't. He drugged you."

Both Jenna and Rumer spoke at the same time. "What? How do you know?"

Ranisha rolled her eyes. "C'mon. I know. Let me guess. He gave you a drink, it tasted real sweet, right? And then you can't remember much. But your body knows. Your heart knows. And you have bruises, right?"

The girls exchanged glances. Rumer didn't want to, but she nodded anyway.

"There still is no p-p-p-proof." Her voice caught in her throat and she swallowed. "It will be our word against his."

A slow smile found its way onto Rumer's mouth. She turned and placed the now folded blanket on Jenna's bed, then took her cell phone from her back pocket. "Not so much."

"I really don't have time for games, Ranisha. I just want to sleep."

Ranisha continued. "Have you seen the video of what happened that day in the club?"

"Everyone has. If you came here to harass her—"

"Let me finish. Have you really looked close?" She brought her screen up so they could see, and hit play. The video from that night began to play.

Rumer cringed. "I don't want—"

"Watch," Ranisha demanded. She let the video play until they got to the part where Rumer began to fall. Dante reached for her, and she stopped it. "Do you see?"

Jenna and Rumer exchanged glances. "See?" They spoke in unison.

"Look closer." She pointed at the screen, then enlarged it.

Suddenly, they were able to see an object falling from Dante's pocket. Ranisha started the video again. He appeared to quickly pick it up and put it back in his pocket. "You see that?"

Rumer sat on the edge of her bed now. "So? I don't see what that has to do with anything. He dropped something and he picked it up."

"He dropped his roofies." Ranisha's voice was deadpan.

"Roofies?" Confusion was all over Jenna's face.

Ranisha groaned. "You really are young, aren't you? Roofies. Another name for Rohypnol. Also known as the date rape drug."

"That proves nothing other than he had some that night."

"Are you sure about that?" Ranisha looked from Jenna to Rumer. She continued. "Do you think that you are the first?" She shook her head as she spoke. "You're not, and neither was I. Dante has done this so many times that his arrogance is legendary. He's pissing people off.

"Once a month, the athlete's lockers are inspected. They're searched. Dante is an athlete—"

"And?" Any impatience that Jenna had been feeling before was replaced by intrigue.

Ranisha smiled again. "When they inspect Dante's locker, they will find his supply of Rohypnol."

Both girls gasped, and then were silent for a minute as that knowledge sank in.

Ranisha raised an eyebrow.

"He's not dumb enough to leave his stash in his locker. I mean, who does that?"

Ranisha shrugged. "You sure?"

"So, how do you know this?" Jenna's voice was low.

"I know. Let's just say I have a friend, a fed up friend."

"Someone Dante's pissed off?" Rumer asked.

"Someone who Dante pissed off. Someone who cares." She paused. "Someone whose sister killed herself after she was raped by

someone she trusted after they put a drug in her drink at a party."
Her words hung heavy in the room for a few minutes.

"So, do you need me to step outside while you get showered
and dressed?" Ranisha's voice was softer now. "You should put
yourself together so we look reliable."

Rumer's body felt heavy as she moved out of bed. "I can't
believe this."

"You should. We're going to go file a complaint, share the
video. Then an hour or so later, they will find what's in his locker."

Jenna spoke up. "But he won't be charged with rape, or battery,
or whatever they charge you with when you drug someone."

"Jenna, it doesn't matter, does it? He'll know what happened
even if he can't prove it. He'll probably lose his job. And there has to
be something you get charged with when you have drugs without a
prescription, right, Ranisha?"

"There is. I've looked it up." Ranisha crossed her arms in front
of her. "This drug is a controlled substance. At the very least, we can
stop him from doing this to someone else. And that's what matters."

Rumer gathered her things and went into the small bathroom
attached to their room. Ranisha and Jenna made eye contact, and
Jenna gave her a small nod, her arms crossed across her body. She
still didn't like Ranisha, nor did she trust her, but she'd been able to
get Rumer up out of bed and on her way to a shower, so Ranisha
deserved a little gratitude for that. Maybe she and her group of
friends weren't that different from them.

"Why are you doing this?" Jenna asked. She felt a little hope for her friend for the first time in days. "I thought you didn't like us."

"This isn't about liking or not liking you." Ranisha paused. "It's about revenge, plain and simple, so don't get it twisted. I'm tired of him making promises and doing this to me over and over. It's got to stop somewhere."

Jenna nodded slowly. "I get it. The enemy of my enemy—"

"Exactly."

Jenna made a note not to turn her back on Ranisha, but she was right. It made sense for them to band together. No one could take back what Dante had taken from her friend, but they couldn't afford to be silent about it. Silence would only make someone else a victim.

CHAPTER TWENTY-EIGHT

Dante leaned back in his office chair and wadded up a sheet of paper from his desk. He aimed for the small, black trashcan in the corner and launched the paper in that direction as if it were a basketball. He knew he had papers to grade, but was having hard time concentrating. He put his feet on the floor and grabbed his cell phone for what must have been the fortieth time in the last two hours.

He dialed Rumer's number again, and just like the last time. It went to voice mail. He didn't leave a message. Instead, he hung up, then immediately texted Ranisha. If Rumer wasn't feeling him, it was her loss. Ranisha, on the other hand, was always down.

"Wanna kick it later?" the text said. He watched as the message turned blue and the status indicator stretched left to right on the top of the screen. The word "delivered' appeared beneath the text. He stared at it, almost willing it to change to "read." When it didn't, he slammed his phone down on the desk, and stood up in the small office. There wasn't enough room to pace, but he took what steps he could, which was exactly four steps in each direction.

A shadow outside the glass of the office caught his eye and he looked up to see Tyrone coming toward him. He opened the door, grinning. His boys always wanted to hang, even if these silly females didn't.

What's up, Man?" He asked. What're you getting into tonight?"

"Me? No plans. I came to check you out and ask you the same thing, even though I know your dance card is full."

"Not tonight it's not. Maybe— "The phone is his office lit up, interrupting Dante before he could finish his sentence. He frowned. "I wasn't sure that thing even worked. "One sec."

Tyrone nodded, and Dante grabbed the phone.

"Dante, this is Dean Jones."

Dante's face flushed. He'd only ever spoke to the head of the Department one other time. Why would be calling? Practically all of their communication had been via email. "To what do I owe this pleasure?"

The dean cleared his throat. "I need a moment. I need you to meet me in in the Men's locker room."

Odd request, Dante thought, but it wasn't like he could refuse. "Sure. When?"

"Five minutes." He didn't wait for a reply. The phone went dead.

Dante held the receiver away from his ear and looked at it. "Dang. He didn't say goodbye."

"Who didn't?" Tyrone asked.

"Never mind. I'm going to have to catch up to you later, Man. I have to handle some business."

Tyrone frowned. "Okay. I know you got stuff to do."

"Walk with me, though. I'm going to the locker room."

Tyrone nodded and fell into stride beside Dante as they made their way down the dimly lit hallway. The locker room was in another building, not far from where Dante's office was.

"What's up with you and Paul?" Tyrone asked after a few minutes.

"What do you mean? Paul's my boy, you know that. We go way back."

"Oh."

"Oh? Dante said. "What does Oh mean?"

"Nothing. I thought you guys had some beef"

Dante narrowed his beef. "No beef on my end."

"Oh."

"Again?"

"Nothing, man."

He had more questions, but no time to ask them. They walked into the athletic building, turned right, and Dante stopped in his tracks. The Dean was in front of the entrance to the locker room, but he wasn't alone. "What the hell?"

"What, man?" Tyrone said.

The Dean spotted him and waved, loping in his direction. His brow was furrowed and he was flanked on either side by city police, with two campus officers right behind him. "Dante, thanks for coming so quickly."

"Is there a problem?" The hairs on the back of Dante's neck stood at attention. Something was definitely wrong. He was no criminal, but he didn't fool with police if he didn't have to.

The dean put his hand on Dante's shoulder. "I'm sure there's not, but we are going to need you to come open your locker."

"What? What for?" Dante backed up.

"I'm sure it's nothing. But we have a complaint against you." One of the city police officers spoke.

"Me?"

"Like I said, I'm sure it's nothing, it's our policy to investigate these things."

Dante relaxed. He knew that he had nothing to worry about. He smiled. "Yeah, no problem. Let's go take a look."

The dean and the officer exchanged a glance, and let Dante lead the way back to the corner his locker was in. Tyrone followed.

Even though he felt he had nothing to worry about, his palms sweat as he tried to maneuver the combination lock. He had to do it twice to get it open. It clicked, and as he opened it, the Police officer's hand shot in front of Dante and grabbed a small plastic bag that was resting on the bottom of the locker.

Dante almost fainted and let himself lean against the locker.

"What's this? The officer said. "I thought you said this guy was legit, Dean?"

"That's not mine. I have never seen that before in my life."

The second officer, taller than the first, took the bag and rolled the white pills in the bag between his fingers, right through the plastic. "Looks like Rohypnol."

Tyrone looked dazed. "Rohip what?"

The officer spoke again, but to everyone in the room. "The

date rape drug."

"I don't nothing about any date rape drug." Dante held up his hands. That is not mine."

The dean's face had gone from purple to almost blue. "We do not tolerate drug use on this campus.

"More like distribution. I know of no one who plans to take rohypnol themselves." The officer's eyebrows went up. "Rarely does anyone take it willingly."

Dante wanted to back up, but there was nowhere for him to go. "I'm telling you, it's not mine."

"Do you know what your Miranda rights are?" The first officer removed his hand cuffs from his belt and grabbed Dante's wrist.

"You have the right to remain silent."

"I'm being framed. This shit is ludicrous."

The officer continued. "I suggest you exercise that silence right." He continued talking to Dante, but he couldn't hear anything he said. His heartbeat was pounding too loud inside his head for him to make sense of what anyone was saying. He was vaguely aware that Tyrone spoke to him as they led him away.

Word had spread quickly. There were people gathered outside the locker room, and Dante barely had time to hold his hand over his face as a camera flashed. Several people held up cell phones, but Dante was too confused to feel shame or anger. He could not understand. He was then man, so how had this happened?

Outside the building, he spotted Paul. He called out to him. "Can you call my brother?" Dante asked.

Paul looked away and it felt as if Dante had been slapped in the face. What in the world?

He scanned the crowd, realizing that everyone would be talking about this later. He didn't care. "Who did this?" he shouted.

He tried to scan to look for someone who would help him. There had to be one of his friends that could do something or call someone. His eyes came to rest on Ranisha. She was standing at the edge of the crowd, as usual with her friends near her. The two of them were alike. They always had a posse.

The policeman opened the patrol car door and put his hand on Dante's head to guide him in. "Ranisha," He shouted. "Call my brother. He'll come get me."

She barely acknowledged him, instead giving him an angry stare. Dante's mouth dropped open in surprise. He was about to say something else, and she stepped to the side.

He gasped. Rumer was standing behind her, dead smack in the middle of Ranisha's friends.

His mouth formed words, but no sound came out of his mouth. "You bitch."

Together, both Ranisha and Rumer nodded back.

DISCUSSION GUIDE

- Early on, Rumer saw evidence that Dante hit Ranisha. How might she have reacted? How would you feel if your boyfriend or girlfriend slapped, punched, kicked, or hit you?

- On more than one occasion, Dante convinced Rumer to change her plans to hang out with him. Do you think that was okay? Do you think he had her best interest in mind? How do you feel about her ditching Jenna to hang out with him? Was this okay? Why or why not? Do you feel that he was monopolizing her time? Why?

- Do you feel Rumer made excuses for Dante's behavior? Was this justified? How do you feel about his flashes of temper?

- When he was a child, Dante's brother told him that it was his job to show women what they wanted, because they didn't know. How do you think that contributed to the way he acted as an adult? Discuss.

- Rumer's mother told her that she wasn't pretty, so she had to work hard to keep a man. Did this impact her relationship with Dante? Why or why not?

- Did Rumer seem to be afraid of Dante? Did she have any clues that she missed about his behavior?

- How do you feel about Ranisha helping out in the end? Did she hate Rumer more than Dante?

- What do you think about Paul's actions? Do you think they were justified?

- Rumer is afraid to come forward and report her experience because she is afraid that she, not Dante, will be persecuted. She compares herself to Hester Primm, from The Scarlet Letter. What do you think of the victim (often the female) being the one that is blamed for these type crimes?

Author Statement

The idea for this book came to life over dinner, in Houston with friends, after the release of my last young adult book, Catfish. My friend thought it was a good idea, but her husband was adamant that it was not. He thought it was a horrible subject to write a book around. The strength of his objection told me that I'd hit on the right thing to talk about. As a mother of two girls, and step-mother to three boys, the "rules" of dating are often a subject that is debated in my house. We hope that our children make good choices and decisions, but the fact of the matter is, they are products of not just our parenting, but the society in which they grow up.

In this book, it was not my intention to paint any of one of characters as good or bad. Just as Rumer was saddled with unintentional learned behavior as a result of the mixed messages her mother taught her in regard to relationships, so was Dante. The ideals he learned about gender roles for men and women helped shape how he treated both males and females.

My intent was not to write a male-bashing story, but instead to make us all stop, think and examine the things we pass on to our young people, and the ways in which we point fingers when these things happen. Too often, we blame the victim and condemn the young men, but like us, these are the same people who have received very strong messages about how they are to go about interacting with the opposite sex. Too often, these messages conflict with modern day values and rules of engagement, and conflict is the result.

Just when does no, mean no and yes, mean yes? The situation in the book is not an unfamiliar one to many of us. One in five teens is a victim of date rape. We hear the little voice in our head telling us to exit a situation, or that something isn't right, but we don't because of fear of embarrassment, ridicule or estrangement from friends. All too often, we see these situations happening, and we neglect to speak up because it is not our business. In addition, it is human nature for both males and females to become enamored with someone in a position of power, and a result, we find ourselves ripe to be taken advantage of. My hope is that And You'd Better Not Tell will act as a microscope on our gender roles and dating behaviors and open the dialogue between young people and adults, as well as males and females, so that we can make better sense of our thoughts and actions around dating and sexual violence.

National Sexual Assault Hotline 800-656-HOPE

Acknowledgements

It gets more difficult to write acknowledgments with each book, not because less people help or inspire you, but because your community of support just gets bigger. This is my umpteenth publication, and I am blessed to say my community is quite large. I could not have written this work without the legal counsel of Cherie Enge, Esq., who was so willing to help me understand what Dante's consequences might have been. In addition, Cassandra Clarke Williams drafted a list of questions for the discussion guide that I was able to adapt to my needs. She is a school counselor at Baltimore Public Schools as well as a Relationship & Wellness Coach. Thanks to both of you.

My Clever Vixen Media family had my back, as always. My assistant, Yolanda Gore read and re-read. My Managing Partner, Barry Jennings, kept my straight and on task, both on the book and at home. Michelle Koike did amazing cover design, Pam Walker-Williams at Pageturner.Net handled my web presence with ease, even when I was a pain in the rear, and Latoya Smith was a bang up editor. Many thanks. My children, Sydney, Kai, Collier, Drake and Ellison walked a wide berth around me when they thought I might be working, and the rest of my family offered absolute support and love; Lynda & Robert Scott and Brandie Smith, I could not have done this without you. Again.

Luckily, or by design, I belong to a fantastic community of writers that inspire me daily, but among them are Reshonda Tate

Billingsley and Victoria Christopher Murray. We really do go way back, and God willing, we will enjoy many more years of friendship. I also have a ton of creative friends who are always the first to buy whatever I'm selling that day. Jami Ervin, Marcea Lloyd, Alma Davenport, Jennifer Silberg, Sarah Potter and Terrance and LLona Gonzalez; you peeps are my ride or die and I love you for it. Thank you to my church members at New Beginnings Christian Fellowship, and my team at both Construction Zone in Issaquah and Save Fitness. Your support means everything. I am also grateful to be part of the amazing and supportive sisterhoods of Jack & Jill Of America, The Links, Alpha Kappa Alpha Sorority, Inc, and The Girl Friends, Inc. Thank you to each and every one of you for spreading the word, recommending me as a speaker or buying a book or a play ticket.

Thanks to Kimyatta Walker for making her daughter read and critique, to Kam And What Not (check out her YouTube Channel) for diving in, and to Ella Curry, Sharon Lucas, The Ladies Sunday Book Club (Seattle), Kindred Spirits Book Club (Los Angeles) and the United California Association of Book Clubs for believing in my work. Finally, no creative work can be successful without those who consume it. Thank you to book clubs and readers alike. I salute you and your love of reading.

Until Next time.

Nina Foxx

Nina Foxx is an award-winning filmmaker, playwright, and novelist. She writes as both Nina Foxx and Cynnamon Foster. Her work has appeared on numerous bestseller lists around the country, and her films have won awards at the Sundance Film Festival, the Tribeca Film Festival, Cannes, and the Rome International Film Festival. Originally from Jamaica, New York, she lives with her family near Seattle, Washington, where she works in Human-Computer interaction for a major software company.

CPSIA information can be obtained
at www.ICGtesting.com
Printed in the USA
LVOW12s0021290717
543051LV00002B/309/P